LEGACY OF SUCCESSION

A DARK SOVEREIGNTY NOVEL

ANNA EDWARDS

Sara
Build a better future
Anna Edwards

www.AuthorAnnaEdwards.com

Cover Design by www.CharityHendry.com
Logo Design by Charity Hendry
Editing by Tracy Roelle
Formatting by Charity Hendry
Proofreading by Sheena Taylor

Legacy of Succession/ Anna Edwards -- 1st ed.
ISBN-13 978-1980484455

"Someone I loved once gave me a box full of darkness.
It took me years to understand that
this too, was a gift."

~ Mary Oliver, American Poet.

ACKNOWLEDGEMENTS

First and always to my great friend, Charity Hendry, for always being there for me. For entertaining my crazy ideas and helping me bring them to fruition. Love you to bits.

To my editor, Tracy Roelle, and proofreader, Sheena Taylor, you polish my books so that they shine brightly.
I'm lucky to have such a good team.

To my street team, thank you so much for all you that you do to get my books out in the reader world.

To Yvonne, for not only beta reading and offering me advice but for organizing so much when it comes to conventions. I'd be lost without you.

To my family, thank you for all the support that you give me.

To Debbie Pothin for naming my Duke in a competition in my Facebook group. Thank you. It's given me so many ideas.

Finally, to all the readers who have embraced me as an author. I'm so glad that you enjoy the stories my mind creates. I hope I'm able to give you many more years of pleasure.

TABLE OF CONTENTS

CHAPTER ONE

VICTORIA

I swear I must have read the same page in this high society gossip magazine at least five times. You know the sort: who's marrying who, which couples are divorcing, and who's running around Chelsea in nothing but their bra and knickers. It's boring! But then again, it's more interesting than the life I have. The highlight of my day would be if the cook changed the strictly ordered meal plan that I've eaten every week, without fail, since I turned sixteen. Five years of the same food is enough to send anyone crazy. But I shouldn't complain. My father, Arthur Cortland Hamilton, Viscount Mayfield, is a wealthy man, and I lead a life of privilege. I've never wanted for anything: clothes, makeup, books, they've all been produced within hours of asking. My days are often spent lounging around by the indoor pool after swimming a hundred lengths, as I am now, but I want something more. I didn't go to regular school like normal people — I was educated at home by a governess. My brother, Theodore, Theo for short, went to a local private school. He would always come home with tales of the friends he'd made and the games that he'd played. My games would consist of reciting my times tables, so I didn't fall asleep from the monotony of the day. I once asked my mother why I wasn't allowed to go to school, and all she would say was 'to protect your reputation'. I have no doubt my gravestone will read, 'Here lies, the honorable Victoria Hamilton. She died from boredom, but at least, her reputation was intact.'

I give up on the magazine and place it down on the

ornately carved sixteenth-century table. I take off the towel, which I'd wrapped around me after my swim. I'm dressed in only a small black bikini. It's the one I always try to choose because of the inlaid embroidery of a rose on it. It's my favorite flower.

"Miss Hamilton?" I turn my head toward the middle-aged butler when he addresses me. He bows.

"Yes."

"Miss Bennett is on the telephone for you." He hands me the phone, and I wave him away before squealing into the receiver.

"Tammy, how are you?"

She's excited about something. I can tell from the hyperventilating breaths coming from the other end of the phone.

"I did it. I've taken my last exam, and it feels so good. I'm sure I passed it. I answered nearly every question."

"I'm so happy for you. That's amazing news."

Tamara Bennett is my only friend. She's the same age as me. We grew up together. She made life tolerable in this mansion of no fun. Her mother, Elsie, is lady's maid to my mother and me. She doesn't know who her father is. Her mother tells her it isn't important. We used to make up stories that he was a hero off fighting for his country, and one day, he would come back for her and Elsie. He never did though, and the truth, about him being a father who abandoned a pregnant woman, seems a lot less exciting. Still, I'm glad she came to live with me because it means I can live vicariously through her. She's been at Oxford University for the last three years, studying law. I've missed her so much.

"All I need to do is pack up all my stuff and I'll be coming back to London."

"When?" I try to temper down my excitement a little bit, but her giggle tells me she knows I'm practically climbing the walls without her here.

"I've got a few end-of-term parties first, so a couple of weeks."

"A couple of weeks," I say sadly.

"I know. It'll go quickly. You'll see."

"I wonder if Daddy would let me come up to see you at the parties? Theo could accompany me. That way, I wouldn't get into any of the trouble he thinks would befall me if I happened to leave the house."

"Victoria." Her answer is ominous. Not because she doesn't want me to come, but she knows my father would say 'no' immediately.

"I just wish for once he would trust me."

"He does trust you."

"He doesn't," I interrupt. "He thinks that if I see a man, who isn't a relative, all my morals will go down the drain, and I'll hump him like a wild dog."

"He's doesn't think that!"

"Then, why didn't he allow me to go to University to study the History of Art? I obtained a place at Oxford. You don't get higher than that. I also had a place at Goldsmiths, which is just down the road, so I'd still be able to live at home. Every time I asked, the answer was 'no'. If he'd trusted me, he'd have let me go."

"He just doesn't want to see any harm come to you. Some parties can get a little bit rowdy." Tammy's voice went quiet on the other end of the phone.

"You've been to them?" I ask.

"A few times."

"What happens, tell me?" My living by proxy is all done through my friend, and I'm not going to let her keep details from me.

"Ria." My nickname since we were toddlers. She struggled to say Victoria when she was younger, so it was just shortened to Ria, and it stuck.

"Please," I beg.

“Ok, there was this one party when I was in my second year. It was after the end of the final year exams. Some of my mates brought in some kegs of beer. They were paid for by one of the final years, he was a billionaire’s son. He had more money than sense. We spent most of the day drinking and ordering in pizza when we got hungry. By the evening, we were all pretty merry.”

“Drunk?” I interrupt, not knowing what that feels like. I’m allowed a glass of wine with my dinner and champagne at the functions Daddy throws. I’ve never been drunk.

“I was on my way to drunk. I wasn’t drunk. My inhibitions were lowered. There was this guy. We’d been working together on our final project for the term.”

“Did you have sex with him?” I know Tammy isn’t a virgin. She lost her cherry, when she was at school, to a guy she’d been dating for a year. She came home and told me all the details.

“Eventually. But first, we played Twister with another couple. Every time someone fell over, they had to remove an item of clothing. You know how clumsy I am. I was naked with my backside in the air in no time. One of the moves put him behind me. He got hard, so we stopped playing and fucked right there on the lounge floor. Most of the party were watching us, but we weren’t the only ones naked. Lots of couples were having sex around us.”

“Wow.” It’s all I can say. I mean I’ve read books about sex and looked at videos on the internet, when I’ve wanted to get myself off, but to be involved in a real-life orgy sounds amazing. Jesus, Tammy had such a good life. “What happened next?”

“Yeah. Next wasn’t good.” She goes quiet. “I found him having sex with some other girl later that evening.”

“The bastard.”

"It was an evening of free love. I went and found another partner."

"I wish I could do it for once."

"No, you don't. Your saving yourself for your husband."

"What husband!" I exclaim indignantly. "Don't I actually have to be allowed to leave the house to find one?"

"Have you spoken to your father again about getting a job?"

"What's the point?"

"You told me about the volunteering position at the art gallery. Maybe since you won't be getting paid, he'll let you?" she asks, hopefully.

"Oh that, I left the information on his desk. I went in the next day and found it in the bin. He wouldn't even entertain it, money or not." I stand up and walk around the pool to the French doors that open over our manicured gardens. We're on the outskirts of London so have a large plot compared to some, and I welcome it because it means I can escape and walk. I open them and take a breath of air.

"I'm sure he'll allow something soon. Maybe when I move back, we can persuade him to allow you to come out with me more."

"It won't happen, there's no point in asking. I'm stuck in this place. Probably until he chooses a husband for me, and then, I'll be stuck doing what another man wants me to do." I'm so down with my life at the moment, I just want to have a purpose.

"We'll think of something," Tammy offers. She knows how sad I get. "What about asking him if you can help him with his business affairs again? He was more than happy for you to help him arrange the functions when your mother was ill. Maybe you could take some of the running of the estates away from her. Talk to her."

"That's a good idea. She's been busy with Theodore and his new business venture recently, and she still looks weak after the flu." Her mother had caught flu the previous winter and had been bedridden for weeks. She had problems with her lungs anyway, from an iron deficiency at birth. It really hit her hard. She spent time in the hospital and took months to recover. "I'll ask him when I next see him. Mother can concentrate on Theo, and I'll run the estates. At least I'll get to talk to people. "

"Great idea." I can hear voices, in the background, on the other end of the phone. They're calling my friend. "I'm going to have to go, Ria."

"Going on another drinking fest?" I laugh, but she goes silent. "Have fun and be careful."

"I'll be home soon, and we'll work on you being allowed out more. I promise. Go talk to your father about the estate."

She hangs up, and I go back to staring out of the window. Our gardens are formal in style. A rose border dominates the vista from the pool. It's June, and the beautiful pink and red petals of the climber's contrast stunningly with the crisp white of the fragrant tea roses. The gardener appears from behind a hedge, and he sees me standing there. I go to ask him to cut a rose for me, but he puts his head down and hurries away back into the depths of the woodland area. Oops, I remember that I'm in a bikini. Awkward.

"Victoria," my father calls me. I stroll back to the lounger and pick up my dressing gown. I've just finished wrapping it around me and tying the cord when he enters the room.

"Father." I smile.

"I've been looking for you everywhere."

"You know I *always* swim at this time," I offer with a

hint of sarcasm, alluding to the fact that I don't have anything else to do.

"We don't have much time." He seems flustered.

"Time for what?" I come over to his side and place my arm through the crook of his. For all my father's overprotective faults, I do love him. I remember once, as a child, him building Theo and me this tent in his office and having afternoon tea with us in it. Theo, of course, being a lively boy wanted to use the shelter as a place to hide from the enemies who were chasing him. He didn't really want to have a girly tea party, but my father insisted that it was my turn to choose the game, we sat with our pinkies out and pretended to drink tea.

"You have to get changed. We're going out."

"Out? Where?" I enquire with a great deal of excitement in my voice.

"It's time," he says and brushes me off, striding away through the house. I follow him as he heads toward my bedroom. Elsie's waiting in the room for us when we walk in. She looks sad. There's a definite air of tension in the room. Elsie steps aside and on the bed is a pure white linen dress. It's plain in design except for a small crest on the breast. I don't recognize it. Are those oak leaves? I try to think to whom it might belong but come up blank.

"Father, will you please tell me what's going on? I'm worried." I take his hand and squeeze it. He looks down at the floor.

"It's time for you to enter society. Put the dress on. No make-up. No undergarments. Just the dress. Elsie knows how your hair should be. We leave within the hour." I stand there in shock. Society? The door slams before I even realize he's left. I get to go and meet people. This is it — I finally get the freedom I crave. Alright, it'll be in probably the most unflattering dress I've ever seen, but at least it's going out. I squeal inwardly with barely contained excitement. My wish is going to come true.

CHAPTER TWO

NICHOLAS

The Ferrari 448GTB, in the obligatory red color, skids to a halt, and I'm out of the vehicle before the footman even has a chance to react. I throw him the keys and stomp into the house. I need coffee, preferably intravenously. I've got a herd of fucking elephants in my head along with a severe case of flashbacks to what was the best twenty-ninth birthday party, ever. Another one hits me when I shut my eyes and slump down into my favorite comfortable chair in the ostentatious room that my father calls the waiting room. It's a blonde this time and a brunette. The blonde is riding my dick like a cowgirl while my friend, Prince John, is doing her up the ass. I've got the brunette on my face, and she's bathing me in her cum. I love a woman's orgasm — it's the sweetest flavor in the world, especially when she's soaking your chin. My dick gets hard again at the thought.

"Down boy," I tell him. "Any more action for you, and you're going to end up with burns. We're taking the day off." I'm sure he's sulking in my pants.

"Lord Lullington." I reluctantly open my bloodshot eyes to see my elderly butler standing over me with the ever-present stern expression on his face.

"This had better be good, Reggie, and it better come with coffee."

"It comes with a bacon sandwich, My Lord." He steps back to reveal the glorious delicacy placed on fine china and resting on my father's sixteenth century, carved oak chest.

"You're sent from heaven." I jump up and sink my teeth into the first juicy bite. "Hmm. Ketchup. This is the best."

"You'll need the strength it gives you." I finish the sandwich in a few bites and pick up the cup of steaming coffee. I know it'll be the King's blend, from Fortnum & Mason, because that's the only one I'll drink since I discovered it at fourteen. I'm not a tea person, unlike the rest of my family.

"Are you going to tell me that my father wants me?"

"He's been shouting obscenities and then your name since the sun rose. He says I'm to inform him the minute you return home." I rub a hand over my unshaven chin and groan.

"I better go and find him before he has an aneurysm."

"It would be wise, My Lord."

Reginald coughs.

"What is it?" I ask, knowing the sudden frog in his throat means he wants to voice his opinion on something.

"May I speak without consequence?" He bows his head.

"Don't you usually around me?" I chuckle and grab my head when it hurts.

"Only when I know you need a bit of fatherly advice."

"Go ahead."

"Don't fight your father on this. You can't stop what's about to happen. It's bigger than anything you know. It's the future of your name and of what governs us."

"Why does it have to be, though?" I sit back in the chair and place my head in my hands. My mahogany hair hasn't been brushed and has a definite recently fucked look.

"History, Nicholas. It's too ingrained in your family to change. To try now would destroy everything. You're implicit in the crimes of the generations past. Blood stains your hands — it can never be cleaned off."

I know that the old man, who's been within my household since I can remember, is right. I have no choice, and I nod acceptance.

"To my death, I go." I get back to my feet and leave him to clear up my empty plate while I search for the man who holds my future in his hands. No sooner do I think of the devil than he appears in front of me, from his office.

"Nicholas, finally. Where have you been?" He stares at me from behind dead eyes. No emotion belies the torture that he's, likely, about to commit.

"My apologies, Your Grace." I've never once called him Father. I was taught at an early age with a wooden cane that he would demand his title, even from his son. "I was enjoying the celebrations for my birthday. I knew it would be the last one I can enjoy as a free man — they may have gone on longer than I'd anticipated."

"You mean that you were sticking your cock in as many women as possible." He raises an eyebrow, which makes me feel like a ten-year-old boy about to get the cane again for stealing a sweet. I'm not, though, I'm a grown man of twenty-nine and should be able to make my own decisions.

"Only two women. My friends shared the other ones."

"You're disgusting," he scoffs.

"Don't tell me you didn't do the same when you were younger, or indeed that you wouldn't do it still, given half the chance." I go to walk away. I've had enough of this. I need a shit, shave, and shower before a long sleep.

"The difference is I do it with decorum and restraint. I don't risk my male parts being posted all over social media with full commentary on how good I am in bed."

"That was one time." I stop and turn back to face him

with my fists clenched.

"And it cost me a good million to silence the little bitch. We have a reputation to maintain, and you're going to throw it all away." My father stands up to my anger, but I'm so livid I'm not about to back down and act sensibly.

"No, we can't damage your reputation as the leader of your little secret society, can we?"

"Jesus, Nicholas, will you grow up?"

"Why? What's the point?"

"Because by your next birthday, you'll be married, the Duke of Oakfield, and the leader of my, 'little secret society', as you put it. This isn't a bad thing I'm asking you to do. I've left you alone, to do as you please with your life, since you turned eighteen. That's eleven years of fun. Do you not find it monotonous? All I'm asking is that you start to take on some responsibility." My father lowers his voice from one full of disappointment and anguish to one I vaguely remember. The one that holds compassion and fondness in it. "You're my son, my heir. I want what's best for you, and I know this is it."

"But why this way?" I state.

"It's the rules. Our forefathers signed the documents governing how we must prove that we're worthy of the title. It's not possible to change them."

"It's possible to change anything if you put your mind to it."

"Not this, Nicholas. There's too much at stake. Oakfield Hall for one."

"This is our ancestors' home since before the time of the society," I protest. "They surely can't take it."

"It was written into the founding documents that all this can be taken from us. The money was needed when it fell into disrepair before your four times great-grandfather came into his inheritance. He was a brave man who was prepared to risk everything for the sake of protecting the name and estates. You can't let him down."

This founding document has been the bane of my life ever since I heard about it, for the first time, at the age of ten. That was when I found out how much my life was mapped out for me. My four times great grandfather needed funds to live. It was around the time that the cost of living went through the roof for the elite, and it became increasingly difficult for them to afford to run a stately home, like the one we now live in. It became even harder for them to pay their way at lavish court functions, which were a pre-requisite for those having a title such as Duke, whether it was a royal title or not. It was necessary to make an appearance, and if the King wanted money then it had to be given to him. Drugs, prostitution, high levels of alcohol consumption, it was all rife then. The elite had to be seen to be partaking. Along with some of the other title holders in the country, my ancestor formed a pact. They'd work together to be able to live the lifestyles they wanted, but in return they had to give up something. My ancestor was designated the leader as he was the highest ranked and also a close confidant of the King. It was decided that should he forfeit his position then Oakfield Hall and any other assets, owned by the Cavendish family, would be sold and distributed between the remaining members of the society. A pretty big forfeiture, considering that in addition he had no say on when or to whom he got married! Because every eldest son on his thirtieth birthday, going down in perpetuity, takes over the title and leadership of the society, on the proviso that he is married. I guess that the position means power and a casting vote in the way the organization's run, but to me, it just takes away my free will.

"Nicholas!" my father shouts at me, and I realize that I'd disappeared into a dream world. "Are you listening to a word I'm saying?"

"Sorry, Your Grace."

"You've been training for this your entire life. You've known it was coming. Think of the power you'll wield, this time next year. You'll be responsible for the business behind the scenes."

"I'm not entirely sure that's something to be proud of." I roll my eyes.

"It is if it keeps a roof over our heads."

"Theft, murder, god knows what else." My father's face reddens as I speak, partly through anger, I think, but also through the embarrassment of knowing that he has the life he leads because of the hardship he puts others through. Actually, no, scrap that. It's all anger because my father doesn't think about anyone else but himself.

"I sometimes wonder what I did to raise such an ungrateful child. Hear me out, Nicholas, enough arguing. You'll shut that intolerable mouth of yours until you can learn to use it for something that's actually important. You'll go to your quarters, and you'll make yourself presentable rather than looking like you have just crawled off the street or out of a barrel of wine. If you don't, you won't like the consequences that I'll be forced to bring down on you." He's seething. The whites of his eyes are showing as he stands face to face with me. My father's a strong man. He may be sixty, but he keeps himself healthy. "The ladies are on their way, and you'll be ready to meet them. You'll show them what it means to be in Oakfield Hall, and you'll embrace your birthright because if you don't then I'll make the decisions for you. I'll make you sit back and watch, while I do your duty!"

My stomach turns — I wish I'd not drunk so much last night. I knew this was coming today, and I knew what I'd have to do. I don't want to marry. I want to fuck my way around England, but my father's right: I have a duty to my family name and my future. Last night was the end of my old life, and today is the first of my new one. I'll embrace the monster that I must become.

CHAPTER THREE

VICTORIA

I stare up at the imposing mansion on the outskirts of London. I thought I lived in a big house, but this place must be more imposing than Buckingham Palace. You can tell that part of it dates back to Tudor times, but the majority of the brickwork and style is gothic in nature, and thus from the Victorian era. I bet these walls can tell a few stories, and I'd love to hear them.

"Hurry up, Victoria," my father calls. I scamper quickly to his side, and we enter together through the grand arch of the welcoming chamber.

"Sorry, Father, I was just admiring the house. Who lives here?"

"The Duke of Oakfield," he replies curtly.

I scan my memory for details on who that is. I've heard that name before — I'm sure of it. Yes, he's the patron of my favorite art museum in London. I'm even more excited for my debut into society because I wonder if he has artwork in his home, which I can study.

The heavy oak doors are opened for us, and we're shown into a room with several other girls wearing the same linen dress as I am. I smile at one of them, but she just raises an eyebrow at me and walks off after a man who must be her father. Fine, I'll avoid her then. My coat and my father's are taken. He's presented with a glass of Champagne. I'm offered one but respectively decline. I want to make sure I remember every moment of what's about to happen.

"Father." He turns to me, when I address him, and

takes a sip of his drink.

"Yes."

"Are we to attend a banquet?" I look around the room at the paintings on the wall while I speak.

"There'll be food later."

"Will gentlemen be attending?"

"Just one."

"Just one?" I repeat and face him.

"The Duke's son, Earl Lullington."

"Oh."

The conversation stops, and my father nods to another man as he walks near.

"My Lord Linton."

"Mayfield."

"Is Lady Joanna ready?" my father asks.

"She's with my wife trying to tame her unruly hair."

"I'm blessed, Victoria has straight hair even if it's as red as a cherry. It must be the Irish blood in Cecilia." I take hold of my hair, which is neatly tied back in a French plait. The end of the braid comes down to my waist. When hanging loose, my hair reaches the middle of my back. I've always loved it long, and the color I find unique. I'm not ginger but a natural dark red. Nobody knows where it came from even if my father blames my mother's ancestry.

"I guess I should blame the Celtic blood for Joanna's curly hair, then. It's as wild as one of the bare-chested brutes who used to run wild over our lands," Lord Linton replies with a chuckle. His attention is taken when a girl the same age as me hurries up to him and bows her head low, so he can see the top of it.

"Is this alright Father," she asks.

He inspects it. Her hair looks fine to me, but then, I don't see why we all need to be dressed the same and so plainly. I don't wear a lot of makeup usually, but I do like mascara and a spot of lipstick. I had all of that scrubbed of my face before I left. This isn't exactly the debut into society I'd dreamed of. I expected lavish gowns, and an evening full of dancing with handsome men. The sort of thing that comes straight from the pages of Pride and Prejudice. Instead, I've got no make-up, no underwear, and a dress that looks like a white bin liner. I pray to god that I don't get it wet because everything will be on display if I do. I can't let a fashion disaster get me down. I'm out of the house — ok, there are not as many people as I expected, but there are still people to talk to.

Joanna's father gives her his seal of approval, and she turns to face me.

"Hello, I'm Lady Joanna Nethercutt," she smiles.

"Victoria Hamilton," I respond.

"The Honorable," my father adds. I never use the title that precedes my name. My father is a Viscount — as his daughter, I am not entitled to use 'Lady' only 'The Honorable'. What's the point? I'm not pretentious. Well having said that, if it were Duchess or Countess, then I'd probably use it.

"Are you excited?" I ask.

"Excited?" She narrows her eyes at me.

"Yes, for your debut."

"We should take our places," my father interrupts and pulls me away toward the front of the room.

"That was rude," I exclaim and look back to Joanna with an apologetic nod.

"You don't need to make small talk and get yourself all flustered. You need to remember your manners and behave." He raises his voice but not so much that anyone else in the room can hear him.

"Sorry, Father." I look down at the ground and wish it would swallow me up. Why do I have a feeling that this evening isn't going to be as much fun as I was hoping for?

My father pulls out his phone and starts to scroll through his emails. I'm dismissed from any further conversation. I take another look around the room that we're in. It's some sort of banqueting hall. Swords, armor, and stags' horns adorn the wood-paneled walls. Any space that isn't wooden is painted cream. There are three paintings on the wall, and I take a step closer to get a better look at them. My father tuts, but I ignore him.

One is a Rembrandt and another a Caravaggio. I'd read about them being bought by a private collector for millions. Wow, the Cavendish family must be loaded if they can afford these. My attention is drawn to the third. I can't place the artist at first, I take a step even closer.

"Victoria," my father admonishes me, but I ignore him again because I can see the signature. Van Gogh's Poppy Flowers. I smirk, knowing that the original of this painting was stolen in two thousand and ten. This must be a fake. I take another quick look at the Rembrandt and Caravaggio. Nothing distinguishes them as fakes at this distance, but given the Van Gogh must be then I'm sure the others are too. The residents of Oakfield Hall aren't as affluent as they like to portray. I stand back and smile, knowingly. It's then that I feel the heat of eyes burning into me.

I turn towards the source of this overwhelming sense of being observed and find a gentleman staring at me. He's tall, about six foot three, and wears a three-piece suit with a crisp white open-necked shirt. His brown hair is long but brushed and neatly gelled in place. His eyes are a cerulean blue like the sky, but a shade darker. He's looking directly at me. My heart flutters, and my breath quickens. I've not seen many men, due to a life spent in relative solitude, but I know instantly that this man screams sex, and by the way he's looking at me, I'm the next delicacy on his menu. I can feel my cheeks heat and want to look away, but I can't. He's captured me in his spell and taken my breath away. He winks and directs his attention back to an older gentleman at his side. They have a similar look about each other, I surmise they must be father and son.

"Victoria, come here," my father orders, and I snap to attention this time. A gong rings out in the room, and the older gentleman steps up onto a makeshift stage. I hadn't noticed before, as I was too interested in the walls, but a fire pit sits on the staging. I can't help but think that a little odd.

"Welcome everyone," the man speaks. "Are we all ready to begin?"

The crowd murmurs a resounding 'yes', and I wait for the music to start.

"For those who don't know me, I'm the Duke of Oakfield and the leader of this society. We're here today to continue traditions our forbearers have handed down to us, for generations." He steps toward the fire pit and pulls out a metal rod. A couple of the men in the room cheer. I look at my father, but he pales and refuses to meet my eyes. "Bring the first one up."

Two men jump down from the stage and take one of the girls by the arms. She screams, "No", but is manhandled onto the stage with little effort. I can feel a heated gaze on me again, and I look to the man who was watching me before. He's watching me again. He smiles — though this time it isn't the sweet one from before but an arrogant one. He steps forward and takes the rod from his father and, without hesitating, brands the screaming girl with a sickening sizzle of burning flesh. I stumble backward, trying to catch my breath, but my father grabs me and causes the world that I know to collapse when he says,

"Your turn."

CHAPTER FOUR

NICHOLAS

My father holds up the arm of the girl who has just been branded. I know her, from the files I've been given about each of them, as Daphne Knight. She's the daughter of a member of the House of Lords. She sobs with the pain, that she must be experiencing, from where the society's crest is forever branded onto her porcelain flesh. I should feel regret, for what I've just done, but I know that I had no choice. I can't show weakness in front of these people who, this time next year, I'll govern. Another girl is brought forward. This one isn't dragged. She comes willingly to her fate. Elizabeth Sandford, a Lord Bishop's daughter, no less. Judging by the fact that she's pushing her lips together in a sexy pout, she's looking forward to what's about to happen. She pulls the material of her dress up and reveals a toned and tanned thigh. She's definitely been preparing. She pulls it a little too high and exposes the edge of a bare pussy. I ignore the blatant flirting and brand her. She whimpers but doesn't break down like the first girl. She has spirit — I like it. I bet she would fuck like a dog in heat.

My father drags the first girl forward to the front of the stage.

"As first declared in eighteen hundred and eight, during the reign of the mad King George III — all girls born to members of the society, in the eighth year after the birth of the son of the incumbent Duke of Oakfield, are to be handed over to the society. This tradition has continued, in perpetuity, down the family lines since that date. My son, Nicholas, has reached the required age, and thus, all girls born in nineteen ninety-seven must be given to us. It's in our ruling documentation and to deny this clause will lead to dire consequences."

I brand another two girls while he speaks. Both sit on the stage, crying tears of pain from the imprint of the society's crest.

"We have five girls here today — five virgins from which my son will choose his wife."

I cringe at that bit of my father's speech. I don't want to marry even if all five of the girls before me are fuckable. I'm a playboy and would rather continue in that vein than be tied to one woman for the rest of my life. A woman who'd most probably hate my guts anyway. Mind you, if my own mother is an example to go by, then my wife is unlikely to be around for long. She died when I was five. They say she slipped while walking on the battlements at the top of the house. I'm not stupid, though. Presuming she'd gone through what I'm about to subject these women to, then it is more likely that she ended up insane and took her own life. My father didn't really care about her death. There was no grief — he couldn't remarry as per the rules of the society, but he could fuck every bit of skirt willing to open her legs for a Duke. The best-case scenario might even be that the woman I marry kills herself before I get her pregnant, and I don't have to subject my children to this ritual crap.

"If any person here doesn't hand over their daughter, then they'll be cast out of the society and all their assets taken away. These are the rules we live by."

The room falls silent. No man will dare go against the society. Nobody of rank within it ever has, and nobody ever will. Money, it's the one thing we all crave, and we'd even sell our daughters just to get it or, in this case, to keep it. The silence is broken when the next girl is called up.

"No fucking way." Her sultry swear has me turning my head toward the commotion. Several of my father's bodyguards, or as I prefer to call them 'hired goons', surround the girl, so I can't see her. "If you think I'm going to let him do that, then you're fucking insane."

Damn, she needs to stop swearing — it's turning me on with the raspy melody of her tone. The guards part when a punch comes flying through the air. I see the vibrant red tresses that follow it, and I know this is the girl who was looking at the paintings. She is exquisite to the eye. All curves and breasts even in the most unflattering dress. Her big eyes are almost emerald in color. I'd immediately wanted to savor her flesh, knowing that it would taste like perfection. But as she's dragged toward me, I see the hatred in her eyes and know that she'll never willingly give herself to me, and I don't take what isn't offered. I don't need to.

"You're all mad. The lot of you. I don't consent to this. My father may have, but I never will. Let me go, or I'll scream so loudly that someone will call the police."

My father laughs before addressing the assembled crowd.

"There's always one who thinks that she's bigger and better than her fate. I don't know why they bother to fight it."

"Fuck you, you freak." She swears again, and my cock lengthens.

"Enough time wasting, we've a long evening ahead of us, and we need to get on with it. Hold her down. Nicholas, the iron. Brand her," my father orders. The men descend on the poor girl, and they grab her hands and legs to pin her to the floor. She has no decorum or grace, at this moment. She's a wild animal fighting for her life.

She's a scared antelope to my savage predator. I stalk her like the ferocious animal I am — a lion hungry for its dinner, and the smell of her fear entices me. Panic overrides modesty, and her sex is bared to me. Fuck, I want her. I'll have her. No, I need to concentrate. I can't allow her femininity to cloud my judgment. I need to succeed. I'm the next Duke of Oakfield. I'll rule this society as soon as I choose a wife. She needs to be shown she's nothing now — a pawn in a fight she can't win. I take the poker and place it hard into the flesh of her thigh. The gossamer skin burns with an acrid smell, and she screams and screams. It's not a cry of ecstasy but one of agony. My throat clenches, and the guilt I feel wraps me tightly in a blanket of disgust. I throw it off, though. She's the one at fault and should just accept her fate. There's no point in fighting what's happening here — it will happen even if we say we don't want it to. Nothing can change what's about to occur — least of all the screams of a girl too young to know better. I look down at her as tears stream from her eyes.

"Stupid girl. You'd be better to accept your fate rather than fight it."

"Go to hell," she whimpers.

I laugh.

"Don't you realize? You just entered hell, and there's no chance of leaving."

CHAPTER FIVE

VICTORIA

The four men holding me let go, and I scramble to my feet. However, not before kicking the freak with the branding iron in the kneecap. The mark inflicted on my skin might only be small, but it hurts so much. It feels as though they've ripped the skin from my body and carved the inside with knives. I tried to cook dinner for my mother once, when I was fifteen, and I burned my hand on the oven. It had barely touched the flesh, but at the time, I thought *that* had hurt badly. Now, I know a lot differently. I move as far away from the staging and all the men as I can. I refuse to let tears fall from my eyes, even though several of the other girls are crying. I won't let them have the honor of seeing my tears. I glare at them instead with an evil stare. If only I had magical powers, they would drop dead in an instant. Has the world I'm living in gone insane? Have I fallen asleep on my sun lounger, and this is a terrible nightmare? Please, let me wake up. I know this isn't a dream when I look at my father. There isn't an ounce of guilt written on his face. He steps forward, signs a document, and shakes the hand of the man who now owns me. I gulp and try to swallow back down the bile forming in the pit of my stomach. The other men handing over their daughters do the same. None of them show remorse. They're clearly happy to commit crimes against the fundamental human right to freedom.

"Nicholas."

The prick who branded me steps forward with a

limp. He bends down and rubs his knee where I kicked him. I wish I could have got him in the balls before he can do any worse damage.

"Your Grace," He addresses his father with a formal title, in a stuck up tone. Ok, it's a deep masculine voice of the type that I might have once dreamed of, but now, I wouldn't touch him with a barge pole. A man's the last thing on my mind. Getting the hell out of this place and as far away as possible from these nutcases, is all I want to do. I survey my surroundings while the men continue to procrastinate and congratulate themselves on being chauvinist pigs. There's the door I came in, but I can't get to it from the stage with the crowd of people surrounding me. There are no windows in this room. What the hell? What kind of place has no windows? Oh yeah, secret society, a room that a bunch of freaks want to keep hidden. I shake my head. I never thought I'd use the language that's running through my head, but I'm pissed off. How could my father do this to me? He's always been strict, but I didn't realize why. I, at least, thought he loved me. He can't if he's willing to put me through this. Does my mother know what's happening? Is she a part of this? She'll be so distraught if she doesn't. Theo, oh god. I don't think I can do this. Despite trying my hardest to keep it in, a tear escapes and tumbles down my cheek. I wipe it away with the back of my hand. I can't allow them to see weakness in me. I tell myself to bide my time. I'll escape this.

The Duke's penetrating voice refocuses my thoughts onto what's happening in the room.

"Welcome, ladies, the next few weeks will decide your future, but before all that, let me introduce you to my son, Nicholas, Earl Lullington. To one of you, he'll be a future husband. To the rest, a nightmare that will haunt your dreams for whatever time you have left." The smile adorning the Duke's face, as he speaks, sends shivers down my spine. How can a man be so evil?

Nicholas stands proudly next to his father with an equally arrogant expression on his face.

"Good evening, ladies. I'm glad to meet you all. Over the next few weeks, you'll be living here at Oakfield Hall and perform tasks to determine which one of you is suitable to be my wife. I have high expectations and will demand complete acquiescence. Any defiance will be dealt with severely. Your mine, to do whatever I wish with. That's the power of my succession. I hope that you'll be able to relax and enjoy yourselves, though."

What, before or after the brand on my leg stops hurting and heals? I think but keep my mouth shut. Now isn't the time to insult my wonderfully hospitable hosts.

"Thank you, Nicholas, we have five girls here. The rules state only three are allowed to enter the final stages of marriage choice. I need you to, now, choose two girls who'll not go any further." My heart starts to beat faster. I have a way out of this nightmare. I can hope he doesn't choose me, and I can leave this place and London. I'm not going back home with my father. I'll go to Oxford and find Tammy. She'll look after me until I can figure something else out.

"Ladies on your feet and form a line for inspection," the Duke orders, and one of the men who held me down comes my way. I'm not going to be manhandled again. I get to my feet and form a line with the other girls. I'm standing next to Lady Joanna Nethercutt. She stands with her weight balanced on the leg not branded. Her eyes are red from crying, but she tries her hardest, now, to suppress the tears.

Nicholas struts over to us with a confident swagger. I want to dig my nails into his eyes and rip the balls from his body. He walks up and down the line, taking in everything about us. When he gets to me, I face him down. I'll not be shown to be weak in his eyes. I'm not a feeble woman as these men clearly think. If he chooses me to stay, I'll make his life hell and not the other way round. He'd do better to get rid of me, now, if he wants the meek and mild little wife, who'll go to his bed willingly, because I never well. Even when hell freezes over. He shakes his head and laughs.

"There are five girls: Amelia, Daphne, Elizabeth, Joanne and Victoria. Which three do you choose to take forward?" the Duke asks of his son.

"Elizabeth," he names the first one, and it figures, she's the bitch who ignored me at the start. They'd make a good couple. Why doesn't he just choose her now, and the rest of us can go home?

"Amelia." A small girl with blonde hair whimpers when her name is spoken. I feel sorry for her but not *that* sorry, since it means there's only a one in three chance of me having to stay here any longer. I can find somewhere with a rose garden and lose myself in the scent. Maybe, I could get a rose tattoo over this thing on my thigh.

"Daphne is free to go." Nicholas states, and the girl screams with delight. Her father curses out loudly — the language coming out of his mouth a complete contrast from the religious ropes he wears.

"So I'm down to two." Nicholas stands in front of Joanna and myself. I think I can hear my heart beating out of my chest. I'm praying my name isn't spoken.

"Victoria you may..." He pauses. Go, say go, I'm pleading within my head.

"Not go anywhere. Joanna's free to go."

I groan long and low with frustration and fear for what comes next. The women named are pushed to the side, and the two not named are grabbed. I try to jostle the guys off Joanna.

"Leave her alone. She wasn't chosen — she's free to go." I ball my fist and punch one of the men. He goes to slap me back, but Nicholas catches his hand and sends him flying off the stage.

"Stop!" the Duke commands, and everyone freezes. He comes up to me and, in a smooth movement, throws me to the floor. I land on my burn, and agony cascades through me. I scream.

"You had to pick the one who's going to cause trouble, didn't you?" he addresses his son with a scowl.

"Why would I want a meek and mild wife when I can have one who puts up a fight?" Nicholas responds, and I try to kick out at him, again. Bastard.

"You..." the Duke addresses me. "Unless you want to spend the rest of the evening locked in the dungeon, I suggest you keep quiet and let me finish this part of the ceremony."

I go to tell him to fuck off, but I think better of it and silence myself with a no-nonsense pout.

"Thank you."

Lady Joanna, Miss Daphne. I'm afraid my son was wrong with his words that you are free to go. You belong to the society now. You may not be in the running to be his wife, but we still own you, and as such, you'll be taken from this place to rooms for rest. Tomorrow evening, you'll be sold to the highest bidder to do with as they please. Take them away."

I gasp, and both girls start to cry. He's going to sell them like slaves. I look to the man who was complaining about Joanna earlier. He's expressionless. This is his daughter — he's going to allow her to be sold to god knows who. I want to scream at him to help her, but when he turns away and leaves the room, I know that it'll make no difference. The men in this room have no respect for women. We're back in centuries of old when women were chattels: bought and sold for gain. I'm pulled to my feet by one of the guards. I don't fight him

— I'm tired and weak. I look over my shoulder to Nicholas. He's watching me be dragged away. He wears the mask of many others in this room. I've died and gone to hell.

CHAPTER SIX

NICHOLAS

"Here is your drink, Sir." Reggie places the fine brandy next to me. I need this, after the events of the day. I want nothing more than to jump in my Ferrari and find a warm pussy to pound away my worries. I know that if I leave the house, my father will have his guards find me and drag me back. These women think they have it hard. I'm just as confined by the damn founding documentation of the society as they are. My head is in my hands, and I rub at my temples. I'm shaking.

"Nicholas, drink it." Reggie urges, and I pick the glass up and drain it in one long gulp. I wonder if the burning in my throat compares to the pain, which I inflicted on the girls' legs. How can I be so callous? It'll be nothing compared to the agony ripping through their bodies that they have yet to experience. Reggie pours me another drink and hands me a cigarette. I'm not a big smoker, but I like one with my glass in the evening. I'm sure it should be a cigar, but a cigarette suffices for me. I puff on the nicotine, killing stick, and the smoke mixing with the amber nectar of my drink starts to relax my body. I wave Reggie away, and he disappears to do whatever task he has next on his list. The man is sixty and should be slowing down, not having to deal with this shit.

I pick up the remote and turn on the televisions in front of me. There are three of them, one for each girl. I look at the one labeled Amelia, first. The guards throw her into her room. She's been washed and provided with a long nightgown to sleep in. You know the sort, the ones that your great-grandparents wore in the Victorian ages. Why we have to continue with the awful fashion, I'll never know. Give the girls one of my t-shirts or some pajamas, anything but those lace doilies for god's sake. I make it my mission, tomorrow, to give them some sensible clothes. Amelia looks around the room, and I notice she's still crying. I wonder whether I should have chosen her or not. She's pretty with her blonde hair and blue eyes. I don't lust after her. In fact, I wanted to protect her more, and that's why I chose her. I knew my father would never let the other two girls go. They know too much, now. The society will own them until the day they die — whether that is sooner or later. I saw strength in them, but in Amelia, I see a terrified little girl who needs someone to watch over her. She climbs onto her bed and pulls the covers over her head. I know she won't sleep a wink tonight not until she's exhausted herself with her tears. A strange feeling of guilt sits on my shoulders. I drink it away with another sip of the brandy and turn off that television. I turn to the one labeled Elizabeth, next.

For a girl who's about to be sold into slavery for the rest of her life, Elizabeth's surprisingly happy about being here. It's the reason I chose her. She's been prepared properly. When the girls are born, they're brought together and christened into the society. Their fathers may raise them telling them of their futures or may keep it a secret. That is their choice, but they must adhere to several rules. The most important being their daughters must remain virgins. If any of them are found not to be, then the girl is disqualified and, from what I've heard of previously, killed. The body is then delivered back to the father who has all his assets taken by the society. What gets me is that nobody has ever talked or gone to a higher authority about what happens here. If my daughter were killed, I'd report it. But then again, my father controls most of the criminal courts in London as well as managing the majority of the government. The culture of fear surrounding us prevents any defectors.

I drink a little more and watch Elizabeth. She, too, wears the ridiculous nightgown but, with a wink to the camera hidden in the wooden paneling of her room, strips it off. How does she know I'm watching? I think she's been a little too well prepared by her father, Lord Bishop of Monchelsea. She climbs into the bed but doesn't get under the covers. Instead, she lays back and parts her legs. I can see everything: her neatly shaved pussy already gleaming with her juices. She runs a finger over her slit from front to back and dips it inside. My cock hardens, but I don't want to touch it. Instead, I make a mental note to check on the validity of this one being a virgin. I turn the screen off and leave her to her intimate act, despite the fact she obviously wanted an audience. I flick the button for the last screen, and the woman who captured my attention in the initial meeting fills it. She's wearing the gown and, apparently, isn't happy with it. I stare intently as she finds what must be a loose seam and pulls it so she can shorten it. The material rips and bares her shapely legs. I find myself leaning forward and hoping she tears too far, and I can get sight of her pussy again. I had a glimpse when she was struggling to prevent herself from being branded. It wasn't bare like Elizabeth's, but it was neatly trimmed. She stops when the gown reaches thigh high, though. Damn it. She goes over to the dressing table and looks at the bottle placed there. We aren't horrible — we make sure that the father's pack a bag of things that'll make the girls feel at home. Victoria picks up a bottle, and I can just make out that it's aloe vera gel. She smears some over the burn and wraps the torn material around the brand. I shake my head at the care she takes. None of the other girls even thought about dressing the wound. It was the first thing she thought of. I'm sure it's some false hope that it won't leave a mark. She finishes treating her leg and takes out the French plait in her hair. Her red waves tumble out, and she sees the brush on the table and uses it to pull her hair back into a neat ponytail. She's exquisite to watch. Calm but with the slight tremor in her hand, I can see her apprehension. I pick up my brandy glass and noticing it's empty, I ring the bell for Reggie. He appears almost immediately and tops me up.

"Are they doing alright?" he asks and motions toward the screen.

"As can be expected," I reply, still engrossed in Victoria. She's looking around the room for an escape route now. She tries the bedroom door — it's locked, and the window is the same. She stamps her foot in frustration.

"Which one is that?" Reggie queries.

"Victoria Hamilton."

"Viscount Mayfield's daughter?"

"Yes."

"She seems braver than your mother. I remember standing here with your father watching her. I'd just been promoted to butler, despite being young. He was laughing at the girls as he watched them cry and try to find their way out. He picked your mother out immediately as the weakest of the three. I knew she wouldn't last long, from that moment." He goes quiet and becomes lost in his private thoughts. I don't ask him to share them. I know he'll clam up. He always does — small snippets about my mother are all I'll ever get out of him. He bows and leaves me alone again.

My attention re-focuses on Victoria. She's at the bookcase. As her fingers skim the titles, she stops on one and pulls it out — I can't make out the name from the angle I have. It doesn't matter because she pushes that one back in when she sees another that captures her attention. I recognize this one. It's a book on art. It's one of my personal favorites, and we have several copies around the house. It lists the more obscure paintings by some of the most famous artists in the world.

She looks between a Queen Anne chair, in the corner of the room, and the four poster bed as she debates on which one to choose. She finally decides on the chair and settles in it with the book. I pull up the file on her, on my phone.

The Honorable Victoria Hamilton
Born: 25th July 1997

I skip past the bit that tells me about her breeding, education, and physical attributes to the hobbies part.

Hobbies:

Victoria swims regularly, at least one hundred lengths a day. She doesn't have many interests that allow her to leave the house as has been specified in the documentation regarding the raising of a chosen girl. She enjoys baking with Viscountess Mayfield and has been painting since a young age. The only time I allow her out, under my strict supervision, is to visit the art galleries of London. She reads an abundance of material on the subject. I'm sure this will be of interest to Earl Lullington.

The passage written by her father does indeed interest me. Art is my life. The pictures in the hallway — she was studying them. I smirk at my intelligent little girl.

Victoria yawns in her chair, and her eyelids flutter. She's becoming exhausted from her long day, no matter how much she wants to continue reading the book that interests her. She yawns again, and her head falls forward. A few seconds later the book drops to the floor open on the page showing Van Gogh's Poppies. I knew it. I turn the screen off and let her sleep peacefully. Tomorrow is a new day, and I think my father is correct: Victoria Hamilton is going to cause a great deal of trouble.

CHAPTER SEVEN

VICTORIA

I'm out at a party with Tammy. We're dancing away to the latest craze, and two guys are behind us with their hands on our backsides. I turn around and lock lips with my man. His deep, raspy voice tells me he wants to fuck me hard tonight. I won't be able to walk the next day. I pull away, and the face of Nicholas Cavendish greets me.

I sit bolt upright in the bed when the door slams, and men flood in, I realize I was dreaming. I'm confused. I'm in bed, but I fell asleep in the chair. I look at the dressing table, and the book I was reading is placed on it. How did I get here?

"Good morning, Miss Hamilton." It's then I realize that the Duke of Oakfield stands at the foot of my bed. My eyes widen as I take in him and Nicholas, plus two other men.

"Get out," I shout.

"Manners. When you address me, you'll call me, Your Grace."

"Get out, you fucking pervert."

I see the little smirk on Nicholas' face, but the Duke's far from having a sense of humor. If steam could come out of his ears, I think it would be right now.

"Playing the little bitch won't get you anywhere." He rips the sheets from my grasp and throws them onto the floor. I'm left on the bed in only the nightgown, which I made shorter yesterday. I'm beginning to regret that decision.

"If you've brought him here to try and take me for

his wife" –I look at Nicholas who is motionless– "then, it'll be rape because I don't consent to this."

The Duke laughs.

"What kind of savages do you take us for."

"Err. The type that kidnaps and brands girls for their pleasure."

He steps forward and slaps me hard on the cheek. I see stars but also see Nicholas' fists clench.

"If I didn't need you pure because my son chose you, I would teach you a few lessons about just what type of man I am, and why you need to respect me," the duke snarls. "This is my private physician, Dr. Fredrick Fallen, and this is my lawyer, Sir Percy Cleveland. When your father gave you to us, he made assurances as to your virginity. As part of the requirements of the rules governing our society, you'll be tested to ensure that is, in fact, the case."

"I'll what?" I pull my legs up to my chest and use the pillow to hide my modesty.

"Don't play dumb. Dr. Fallen here will check to see that your hymen is still intact."

"Hell no." I scramble from the bed and grab the nearest implement to protect myself. A lamp. "If any of you try to come near me, Dr. Fallen will need to spend his time stitching your head back together rather than sticking his fingers up my vagina."

The Duke sighs, "Nicholas, why couldn't you have chosen the docile one?"

"Less fun to break," he replies and steps closer to me.

"Try it, and there won't be anyone for us to marry."

He picks up the book on my table instead.

"Interesting book choice." He opens it to the page that shows the Van Gogh painting. It's then I realize he was the one to move me. I do a mental tally in my head to see if it feels as though I've been violated anywhere. Maybe he drugged me.

"You get your kicks from sneaking into a sleeping lady's room? Mind you, it's probably the only way you can get someone near that small dick, your no doubt packing."

"My dick's the thing of your dreams, Victoria." He gives me an arrogant grin.

"Get a life." I roll my eyes.

"I've got three to play with at the moment, thank you."

"Enough." The Duke interrupts our bickering. "Guards."

Four men file into the room.

"We don't have time for this. We need to see the other two girls, and then, we have the sale. Disarm her and hold her down."

"Is that the only way you can get a woman?" I make a swing for the Duke, but one of the guards rips the lamp from my hand. The others grab for me, and I'm dragged, kicking and screaming, toward the bed. I don't want this. I want to disappear back into my dream, preferably without Nicholas Cavendish in it. Actually, no, I could happily be dreaming of him and his father getting castrated. Instead, I'm thrown face down on the bed. The guards each pin one of my legs and arms down. I thrash my head around, trying to shift enough to sink my teeth into flesh, but a massive hand pushes it down so I can no longer move. I flick my eyes up to see that it belongs to the Duke. He's sadistic in his triumph over me. I feel my hips lifted and my gown pulled around my waist, bared to the eight men in the room. My ass in the air like a wild animal ready for the taking. Nicholas comes to the head of the bed. I watch his every move. He's like a stalking lion, surveying his prey. He plays with the cufflinks that peep out from his suit jacket. They are gold in color and emblazoned with the symbol, which will forever scar my skin. In this position, I have no dignity, and he's enjoying it.

"Don't fight — relax, and it won't hurt so much." He orders. I spit at him in a fury, and he wipes it away with a smirk. His eyes never leave mine as two fingers are inserted into my body. I experience severe pain because I'm dry and not prepared — the doctor is tearing me apart. I screw my face up, but I can't take my eyes off Nicholas'. I want him to die, painfully, slowly, and maybe, with two fingers stuck up his ass. No, make that a whole fist.

The doctor gropes around inside me, and I can't help but feel violated.

"She's a virgin," he announces and withdraws his fingers. I breathe a sigh of relief. Nicholas looks pleased.

"I could've told you that without the need for all of this." I try to struggle, but they still hold me down.

"Give her the injection." The Duke's voice comes from behind me. There's silence for a few moments except for the movement of the doctor, and then, I feel a sharp jab in my bottom. Everyone holding me lets me go, and I scramble as far away, to the other side of the room, as possible.

"What did you do to me?"

"A contraception injection. No babies before marriage allowed here. It wouldn't be proper," the Duke answers me.

"Proper? After what you just did, you're talking to me about what's proper and what isn't."

The Duke ignores me.

"Is there anything you can give her to calm her down a bit? Her constant moaning has given me a migraine and become far too tedious." He glares at me, but I stick my tongue out and look for another weapon. If any of them come near me, then they're going to lose their heads.

"Leave her, Your Grace," Nicholas interrupts. "I think

that when she sees what happens next, she'll behave." He turns on his heels with no further explanation and leaves. The Duke looks at me and cackles, making my blood freeze, and my body slump to the floor in defeat.

CHAPTER EIGHT

NICHOLAS

I watch the girls file into the room. Those to be sold are led to the stage while the ones I chose to keep, for now, are being ushered to seats and told to sit. I watch them. Elizabeth's her usual confident self and flashes a seductive smile in my direction when she walks in. Amelia's barely holding it together — she seems like she's a zombie. Victoria's quieter than usual. I think I'm getting used to her having a mouth on her and miss the backchat. She doesn't curse the guard who pushes her down on the chair, and I notice she's walking a little stiffly. She struggled a lot this morning. Her muscles must be hurting from the exertion. She needs to learn to go with what's happening here. Nothing can change the future.

"Welcome back, gentlemen." My father starts proceedings with his confident address. The room instantly silences, and we all focus our attention on him. "Let's get straight down to business. We have two ladies here, Lady Joanna Nethercutt and Daphne Knight. I'm going to start with Miss Knight. Daphne step forward please."

The small brunette does as she's told — her eyes are red-rimmed with tears. What is it with all these women and tears? Why don't they just accept what's happening and get on with it? None of us have a choice in this farce. At least they'll have a roof over their head at the end of it. There are plenty of people on the streets of England who have nothing. That's what we all fear, after all, nothing — no life, no wealth, no love. I snort at the last one. Oakfield Hall has never had any love within its walls.

I look over at Victoria again. I can see her cheeks are flushed red — she's getting angry. I find myself wanting her to scream and shout and interrupt the proceedings. I like her spirit. She must feel me watching her because she turns her attention in my direction. She rolls her eyes in derision. I smirk, and she focuses back on the sale.

"Daphne's an accomplished musician. She plays a variety of instruments including the piano, violin, and harp. She's been privately educated to a high standard and particularly enjoys reading classics. She'd make a good governess and tutor for the next generation of our society." My father pauses and Laird McGuire, a despicable man from the Scottish Borders, calls out.

"Enough with the tedious facts. What aboot the interesting ones. How big are her boobs? I'm assuming ye've checked she's a virgin. A dinnae want sloppy seconds from yer son."

"Laird McGuire, I can assure you that she's been checked and is innocent. Her vital statistics are in the pack, which you were handed on arrival." My father doesn't like this man. In fact, he has a thing against most Scots. He believes them brutish and uncouth. I hear him often chastising my ancestors for allowing them into the society. Thankfully, Laird McGuire and Laird McDonald, who is also loud but less of an oaf, are the only two of Scottish origin.

"A bet she takes a good whipping. Her skin is pasty white. Will color red in a matter o' moments. A think I'll be bidding on this one. Get ma cock up her ass within the hour and fuck her senseless."

Daphne lets out a whimpering cry at his comment, and Joanna steps forward and holds her up.

"Laird McGuire. These are ladies, not whores. Please,

have some decorum if, that is, you intend to place a bid on Miss Knight. If you simply want a body to engage in sadistic acts, then my butler will provide you with a number to contact."

"We have a right to bid on these pieces of meat. Ye canae be telling me how to treat them." Laird McGuire is on his feet and waving his fist at my father.

"No, I can't tell you how to treat them, but I can outbid you and see that you don't win."

I chuckle under my breath. My father doesn't want this girl. He doesn't care what happens to her. If he did buy her, he'd be the one fucking her up the ass within the hour. He just wants to put this man, that he hates, in his place.

"Should we continue, Your Grace."

I step up onto the stage and link my arm around Daphne's. Her legs are weak, and she leans on me.

"Please, don't sell me to him," she whispers to me.

"You'll be sold to the highest bidder, no matter who it is. Those are the rules. Accept it," I reply heartlessly.

My father comes to stand on the other side of her, and Laird McGuire sits down with a scowl on his face.

"Shall we start at one hundred thousand?" my father offers to the crowd.

Laird McGuire puts his hand up.

"Two hundred thousand." Comes from Earl Winters, an older man with a penchant for young girls. He's kind though, and she'll be treated like a princess. He has a daddy complex. Don't get me wrong — he'll fuck her, but she'll be looked after.

"Three," Lord McGuire counters.

"Four," Winters offers in reply.

"Five," A new voice enters the fray. I don't recognize it at first but purse my lips in a smile when I see that it's one of my old friends, Viscount West. This just got interesting.

Lord McGuire waves his hand in defeat, and my father smirks with triumph. West must be bidding on his behalf. Fuck, the poor girl's screwed.

"Earl Winters?" my father asks.

"Five and a half."

"Six." West counters right back.

"She's not worth anything more. I'm out." Earl Winters accepts defeat, and the hammer comes down on Daphne Knight. I can't help feeling a little sick. If my father has anything to do with this purchase, then the girl wrapped tightly around my arm has little time left to live. There's nothing I can do, though. I hand her over to West and go to the next girl.

Lady Joanna Nethercutt was a difficult one to give up. If Victoria hadn't intrigued me as much as she did, then I would have chosen Joanna. She's the prettier of the two. All I can do is pray that McGuire has learned his lesson and won't try to bid on this one.

My father gives the same speech about the girl again. This one is again highly educated and enjoys reading. She's also an avid motor car fan. I picture her laid out over my Ferrari. It would be a damn good sight.

"What shall we start at?"

"Two hundred." Earl Winters puts his hand up again.

"Three hundred," Laird McGuire replies, and I groan.

"Four." Viscount Mayfield steps through the crowd. Victoria gasps when she sees her father.

"Five," McGuire offers.

"Six," Winters adds.

Victoria is shaking her head. She has tears in her eyes, now. Mayfield bidding isn't something I'd expected. I know his wife came from my father's 'not chosen' girls. I wonder if he's continuing the tradition.

"Seven." He stands in the center of the room with his arms folded.

"Wit that frizzy hair I'm no paying any more. Ye can

have her." McGuire gets up and stomps from the room.

"Eight." Earl Winters comes forward to stand next to my father.

I'm on edge as to where this is going.

"One million," Mayfield responds.

Earl Winter's shakes his head in defeat.

"Sold to Viscount Mayfield," my father shouts out.

Victoria gets to her feet and is running toward her father before the guards can stop her. She pulls her fist back and punches him square in the jaw.

Joanna, who has been standing quietly until this moment, screams and falls to her knees. She fears the worse.

I jump down from the stage and pull Victoria off her father. She's swearing and shouting at him still.

"You bastard, how could you? I hate you. I want you fucking dead. If you hurt Theo, I'll hunt you down and kill you myself." She's struggling in my arms. She doesn't even realize I'm holding her. All she wants to do is scratch her father's eyes out. She makes some ground when my dress shoes slip on the floor. I regain my footing just as she goes to pull another punch.

"Stop it," my father shouts, but she doesn't listen. Two other guards pull her away from me and flatten her to the ground. She's trying to kick out, but they use their weight to keep her in place.

"Viscount Mayfield, take your purchase and go," my father orders.

Victoria's father looks down at where she's being manhandled on the floor. I don't know about his daughter wanting to punch his lights out, but I'm struggling to keep the lid on my composure. My fists are balled, but I'm not moving. I can't.

He shakes his head.

"I thought she was brought up better than this, Your Grace. I'm embarrassed. Punish her as you see fit." I'm walking closer to Mayfield when he speaks. I have my hands on the collar of his shirt, and I'm dragging him away.

"The Duke said leave," I order with spit flying into his face.

"Theo," Victoria screams from the floor.

"When she regains her composure, tell her that I'll never hurt my son. Lady Joanna is to be his wife. It's a family tradition — for the procreation of the next generation."

"Get out!" I'm inches from the Viscount's face. I have no further words for this man. He disgusts me. Violence is the only way that I can express what I feel.

"Nicholas," my father commands me, and I step away. The Viscount and his purchase leave. The other members of the society who attended the sale also start to file out. I go to the side of the room and calm myself. I can still hear Victoria's small whimpers for her brother.

"Well, after all that excitement, I think we need a rest before tonight," my father addresses the two girls who are still seated. "Ladies, during your stay you have free rein of the house, except for the second floor. Those are private quarters for myself and my son. If you are caught there, you'll be punished. Please make yourself at home. We have a society meeting tonight, and you'll be expected to join us. I'll have garments and instructions sent to you later. In the meantime, enjoy your day. Cooks are available for your particular diets. We have a pool in which you can swim. However, the gardens are off limits, at present. Please go." The two ladies get to their feet and shuffle out.

"What do we do with her?" one of my father's guards asks and points to Victoria.

"Put her in her room. She gets the same treatment as

the other's, unless Nicholas decides she needs punishment."

I spin on my heels to face him.

"Punishment?" I question.

"If she's to be your wife, then she should show more decorum. I'm beginning to think she doesn't know the meaning of the word with her outbursts."

My father's testing me. He's never thought me strong enough to be his heir. I'm the only option, though. He would never choose... I shake that thought from my head.

"Place her in her room and lock the door until this evening. No food."

"Yes, Sir," the guard replies and pulls Victoria to her feet. She purses her lips at me, and I can see the curses flashing through her brain. She's imagining me boiling in a vat of oil. She's imagining bringing down the whole society.

"Wait." I stop them as they begin to pull her away.

"Make sure you remove all the books from her room. She's to think on her behavior."

"You bastard," she spits at me.

"Learn your lesson, little girl."

I turn and walk away as she continues to call me names.

CHAPTER NINE

VICTORIA

I've spent most of the day pacing my bedroom. I've searched again, four times to be precise, for an exit from this house. Everyone here's completely insane. My father bought a girl for my brother — my mother was paid for, by him, and I was bred purposely to go through this fucking charade. My head is a mess, and I just want to sleep, but I know that it'll never come. I'm in an endless nightmare, but not the sort where there are monsters under your bed. No, I'm in the type of horror where the monsters are real and controlling my future like I am a puppet on strings. Future — do I even have one? My stomach lurches. What happens if I'm not chosen? God, do I want to be selected? At least I know the devil I'll be with. I think back to the Scottish oaf who was trying to buy the girls. The thought of being sold to him would kill me. Literally, I imagine, after he's used my body in ways that no woman should have to suffer. I need to try and get my head together. I'm hungry. Nicholas banned me from having food today, and for the last hour, my stomach has protested his decision. I'm not going to let him beat me though. No fucking way. I'd rather die...I stop that line of thought again because, here, it's too real a possibility. Maybe, I should just keep quiet tonight. Do whatever it is they have planned and come back to bed and sleep. Sleep will make my head clearer, and if I can explore the house tomorrow, I might find a way out or, at least, get my books back.

I dress in the white gown they've left out for me.

This one is silky and not like the white dress that was provided for my arrival. A maid comes into the room and ties my hair back in what seems like the requisite French pleat. I ask her if she's able to tell me what's happening tonight, but she doesn't reply. I guess they're allowed to make us look pretty but not actually talk to us. How can they let us go through this? Clearly money speaks louder than kidnapping and rape.

At precisely eight in the evening, I'm led into a banqueting hall with the other two girls. Amelia looked awful this morning but seems much calmer now. Elizabeth looks her usual stuck-up bitch self. I don't like her in the slightest. We're brought to stand at the head of the table where the Duke sits. Nicholas sits to his left-hand side in a formal dinner suit. It looks good on him. I chastise myself for even thinking that.

"Welcome, ladies." I look over the table. There must be at least forty men sitting around it. I recognize a lot of faces from functions my father has had in previous years. I look for him, but he isn't here, thankfully. I'm not sure I'd be able to behave, as I promised myself, if I had to watch him continue to act like a man who deserves to have his balls chopped off with a machete. The men range from their early thirties to late eighties, in age. I guess they're the men of title within each family. When one dies, another inherits and takes his place in this society of freaks. I memorize each face. One day, I'll get my revenge on them.

"As you can see, we have a meal here tonight to celebrate my son's birthday, and the start of his journey into his succession. You are joining us as his prospective brides. Our society needs a strong woman to stand at Nicholas' side. He will become the greatest leader we've ever had — I'm sure of that. I've taught him everything he knows, after all." The Duke laughs at his joke, and everyone joins in. Eventually, he holds his hand up to silence them. "Over the next few weeks, to help Nicholas choose between you, you'll be given tasks to complete. Tonight is the first of those."

He gestures to where three marble plinths stand at the other end of the table. I hadn't noticed them before, but they suddenly feel rather ominous and are the only things I can focus on. Our guard ushers us down to the marble stones. I'm naked under my dress, and I can foresee what's going to happen. No fucking way am I going to stand here, while they eat, in just a dressing gown, or, as I suspect, without it!

"Ladies, remove your dressing gowns and stand on the plinths. We're getting hungry for our dinner and can't start until you are in place."

Elizabeth eagerly removes her cloak and jumps up. She juts her hip out to emphasize the curves of her body. Amelia, like me, stands with the gown pulled closely to her chest.

"Nicholas!" The Duke's voice booms from the other end of the room. The Earl stands and comes over to us.

"Ladies, remove your gowns, or I'll do it for you?" His deep voice is commanding in an 'I want to punch him in the head' way.

Neither of us moves. He takes a step closer to Amelia, and she instantly panics and drops the gown. She's up on the plinth, in a matter of seconds. She stands with an arm over her chest and a hand covering her lady parts.

"Hands at your side."

She shakes her head

"Please," she whispers.

"Sides," he demands again. I want to tell him to leave her alone, but I have to behave. I don't want to be naked, but I do want to be allowed out of the room, relatively unscathed. She reluctantly drops her arms.

"You have nothing to be ashamed of. You have pretty breasts, but I think I'll send someone in to wax your pussy tomorrow. I prefer a little less hair on my women."

I can't help but look and see she has a bit of a bush thing going on down there.

"Sorry, my father wouldn't let me cut it," she stammers.

"Not a problem," he responds and turns to me. "I'm not even going to ask you again to remove your gown because I know the answer will be 'no'." He steps forward, and before I know what's happening, the material lays in tatters on the floor.

Any thought of behaving goes out of the window when I spit in his face. He wipes it away with a smirk.

"If you want to swap salvia, I have a much better way of doing it. Now, get up there and behave." He looks me up and down with a lick of his lips. My skin heats in a good way. What the hell? I jump up on the plinth and put my hands at my side in the hope that he'll go away.

"Good girl."

I stick my tongue out at him when he walks away. It's childish but the only retort I can give.

"I have better uses for your tongue as well," he shouts over his shoulder. How did he know?

"Go to hell," I shout after him.

He turns and faces me. The playfulness, which was on his features moments ago, is gone. His eyebrows gather in, and he closes his eyes,

"I'm already there. Haven't you recognized it yet?"

His eyes flash open, and there's pain written in the blue hues of his irises. I don't respond — I'm too shocked. He returns to his seat, and to the congratulations of the men.

"Ladies, as my son's property, only he is allowed to touch you intimately. You have no say in the matter, and it'll serve you to learn that lesson quickly. The courtesy is also extended to me as the ruler of the society. The others at the table are allowed to touch you but not between your thighs, unless expressly given permission."

I snort quietly. If any of them try to touch me, I'll break their bloody hands.

"Miss Hamilton, do you have something to say?"

Shit!

"No, Your Grace."

"Oh, come on," he chuckles. "I'm sure the entire table would love to hear your feelings on what's wrong with the world."

"The world's fine. It's the people in this asylum that have lost the plot." Me and my stupid mouth. Why won't it be quiet? Shush, I tell it. We want to escape so we need to behave.

"You feel my household is suffering from some kind of insanity." He pushes his chair back and comes toward me. Keep your goddamn mouth shut, I tell myself. Of course, it doesn't work.

"Well, I'm pretty certain normal people don't buy and sell girls."

The Duke stands in front of me now.

"I think you'll find that it was your household that did the buying and the giving away. What am I supposed to do with five pretty girls? I'm just following the natural law of things."

"You're a freak who will get his comeuppance one of these days."

The Duke reaches out and grips me tightly around the throat. The plinths are low, so I'm at the perfect height for him to grab. I can barely breathe as I feel his strong fingers squeeze tighter around my slender neck and lift me off my feet.

"Your Grace." Nicholas pushes his chair back with a

loud scrape on the tiled floor.

"Sit down, boy."

"She's mine to punish, not yours."

The Duke drops me, and I tumble back down onto the plinth, gasping for breath. He turns to his son. I can't see the look on his face, but I can feel the tension in the air.

"Sorry, I got ahead of myself for a moment." The Duke faces me again and holds his hand out. I reluctantly accept it and allow myself to be pulled to my feet. Big mistake. The Duke pulls me toward him with a caress to my breast. I want to tell him to get off me, but the look on Nicholas' face distracts me. The pain is back, and there is jealously intermixing with it. He wants to stop his father, but he knows, on this, he can't. This is all a game between him and the Duke. I'm just a pawn in the middle. Can I use that to my advantage?

I step quietly back onto the display stand. I hold my body straight. Years of deportment lessons come in handy. The Duke goes back to his seat at the table, and the entrée is brought in. Elizabeth, Amelia, and I stand there while the food and wine flows at the table. The chatter of the men fills the room. I can here talk of conquests with ladies, discussions about business deals, and I take it all in, learning everything possible, so that I can prepare my fight. I'll not submit to these people without starting a war between them all, if necessary.

The main course is cleared away, and several of the men, now a few glasses of the finest claret down, turn their attention to us ladies. I want to cut their eyes out with the cheese knives that are being placed in front of them, on the table.

"Gentlemen, you may inspect my son's acquisitions if you wish. It's in the rules that you can touch them. Just remember between the legs is off limits." The last words the Duke speaks are said with a snide smirk at his son.

I brace myself as the men slide back their chairs, causing as eerie scraping sound from the floor. Stay calm, I tell myself — you can get through this. Hell, who am I kidding? I've never been naked before a man in my life, and now, I'm in front of forty plus men looking at me as if I'm a popsicle on a stick.

One of them, a man in his fifties with a comb over and greasy appearance, steps forward toward my plinth.

"Her tits are far too small. Nothing to play with." He flicks his hand over my breast and pinches the nipple. I ball my fists at my side, knowing I can't move. If I do, I'll hit him, and I'm actually too scared to find out what the punishment for that would be. Someone runs their hand over my backside.

"This is pretty good though." He pinches a cheek. "Nicholas, I bet she takes it great up the ass." He calls over to the Duke's son, who's sitting forward in his chair. His whole body is rigid with tension, and, it appears, he can't bear to look our way. Prick!

The man runs his hand around the lower half of my body. I feel sick, sitting at the back of my throat, but I'm pretty certain that if I hurl on him, it's going to cause problems. He stops his hand just inches from the 'v' between my legs. All of a sudden, he's pulled aside.

"Too close," Nicholas snarls at him.

"I wasn't going to break the rules, My Lord."

The bell rings to signal the next course. The man who had his hands all over me returns to his seat. Nicholas looks up at me.

"Turn around," he snarls.

I go to open my mouth but think better of it and spin on the plinth.

"You two as well," he orders Elizabeth and Amelia. He stomps back to his seat, and the cheese course is served. I don't know if not facing the men is better, or not. I can feel my body shake. What kind of hell is this?

Will I survive it?

CHAPTER TEN

NICHOLAS

"Can I get you anything else, Sir?" Reggie pours my second cup of coffee while I finish off the bacon with a poached egg that I always have for my breakfast.

"No, thank you — I'm full." We have the same exchange every morning. I sometimes think I should ask him for an apple just to alter the monotony of the conversation. "Are any of the girls awake?"

"I believe Miss Sandford has called for breakfast in her room today. She's apparently suffering from that 'time of her month' and needs to rest. Miss Amelia has been for a swim and is eating a croissant in the ladies' dining room."

"What about Miss Hamilton?"

"Miss Hamilton has been confined to her room."

"On whose orders?" I place my knife and fork down and look up at him.

"Mine, Sir. She was up early and looking for ways to leave Oakfield Hall. I'm afraid the guards found it rather tiresome after the third escape attempt, so I ordered her to be taken back to her room."

I shake my head and laugh.

"That woman will be the death of me."

"I have a feeling she may be the death of a lot of people before you make your decision," Reggie replies with a shake of his own head.

"Does she have any reading material left in her room?" I ask.

"You've not given me orders to have it returned yet."

"No, I haven't. I tell you what. Have one of the guards escort her to the pool. In her manifesto, it said that she likes to swim one hundred lengths a day. Have them tell her that if she swims that amount, then she'll be rewarded with the return of her books. If she defies, or tries to escape again, then all the furniture will be removed from her room. Hopefully doing something energetic will tire her out a little and placate her."

Reggie motions to look out the window.

"What?"

"I thought that I saw a flying pig, Sir."

"She does provoke that reaction." I push my chair back and go to stand, but I am interrupted by my father's gruff voice from the doorway.

"Who does?"

Reggie looks at me.

"Miss Hamilton." I reluctantly concede, knowing that there's no point in lying to him.

"What has she done now?" He stomps over to his seat at the head of our small family dining table and sits down. Reggie steps forward and pours him coffee. My father doesn't say thank you.

"Nothing of concern, Your Grace. It's been dealt with." I finally get to my feet and bow to my father with the intention of taking my leave. He doesn't let me go, though.

"Why you had to choose her to continue on, I'll never know."

"She is different from the other girls. I don't know what I want in a wife, yet. I chose the girls that all offer me something unique in the hopes that I make the right decision for the society," I offer in reply.

"She deserves to be tied to a bed and fucked raw."

"If I choose her to be my wife, then I'll make sure I do that."

My father takes a long sip of his coffee.

"She spoiled my fun last night. Having one of the girls was my right, and you left me with one who just lay there and took it. She didn't even scream once."

"Daphne Knight?" I enquire with a hint of frustration in my voice.

"Don't get all high and mighty with me. You knew full well what would happen to her and the other one, when you didn't choose them." Reggie steps forward as my father speaks and places a napkin over his lap. "Full English breakfast, Mr. Hane."

"Of course, Your Grace."

Reggie disappears into the kitchen as fast as his tired legs can carry him.

"Is she still alive?" I ask.

"I don't always kill them." My father purses his lips in disgust.

"No, just leave them completely broken." I want nothing more to do with this conversation. A woman is a precious thing and not there to be beaten to a pulp while you get off in her pussy.

"She was fine when West took her."

"Did he fuck her as well?" I'm fuming.

"She has more than one hole — so of course he did," my father chuckles. I want to rip his head off. "Don't start having morals now. Everything that's happening here is for you and your future. Grow a pair of balls and man up." My father turns his evil eyes on me. They bore into my soul and deny me any hope I have of being innocent. Daphne Knight was brutally raped and beaten last night. She's probably lying dead in a gutter somewhere because of me. I can't change what's happening, but I can try to soften the blow for the three girls left. Once I make my choice, two more will be sold. I can only save one girl and bring her in to the hell I live. At least there, as my wife, I can protect her.

"You and that piece of paper may govern the tasks

the girls have to perform, but it doesn't tell me everything that I should do. I'm going to spend time with each of the girls today — a date around the property."

My father lets out a rambunctious laugh.

"What's the point? You just need to marry her, fuck her, and stick a male heir in her belly. Then, once she has given birth, she can go up in the rafters of the house and descend into the kind of obscurity that is only found at the sharp end of a heroin needle — just like your mother."

I step back because I'm on the verge of punching my own father. I can feel my blood boiling with fury, and my hands shaking. I take hold of the back of a chair to ensure that my hands are gripped tightly around something, other than my father's neck.

"Actually, Father" –I stress the alien word with venom– "I would like a loving Mother for any children I have, not a drugged up waste of space like my own was. You always tell me that I'm a disappointment to you. Maybe, if I'd had a caring mother, I might actually have ended up as much of a bastard as you are."

I don't wait for his reply. I don't want to hear it. I'll take the girls out and get to know them better. I'm bound by the document that prescribes my future, but I don't have to do everything the way my father wants. If I'm going to have to marry, I'm going to make sure that it's with a woman who won't be a mess by the time she pushes out my first child. And fuck, I need to look into ways to make sure that any children we have are girls, so, hopefully, I can end this whole sordid charade.

CHAPTER ELEVEN

VICTORIA

A date? The freak wants me to join him for one on one time. What? Is this where he takes our virginity and sees which he likes best? If he thinks that he's getting into the panties, they've finally provided me with, then he has another think coming. I'd sooner chop his bloody dick right off. I bet it's microscopically small and riddled with infections. Covered in warts from all the whores he, no doubt, has shoved it in. I bet the 'virgin' and 'hidden away' clauses haven't been applied to him. All these men are chauvinist and think they can get away with rape and murder. Well I am going to be the one to change all that. I throw the book on 'decorum for a lady' down on the table. I swam a hundred lengths this morning with the promise of books, and I get etiquette ones. Bastard, and a few other choice words, that a lady isn't supposed to know, start to spill from my mouth, but I'm interrupted by a knock on the door. I don't bother to tell whoever it is to go away. They'd probably just remove the door and leave me exposed to everyone if I did that.

"Come in."

One of the guards assigned to me comes in.

"Earl Lullington requests your company in the sitting room."

"Tell him I'm busy studying his etiquette books," I reply without even looking up.

"Maybe I should rephrase my instruction. Earl Lullington wants you in the sitting room. If you refuse, I have orders to drag you there" –he licks his lips when I scowl at him– "by the hair, if needed."

"Well, why didn't you say so?" I reply sarcastically. Getting to my feet, I slip on a pair of ballet pumps. "We must go immediately. I wouldn't want to keep the Earl waiting for a moment. He's just such the gentlemen and his manners..." I roll my eyes.

"I hope he doesn't choose you," the guard replies, and I stop in my tracks.

"What? Scared I might actually be the one bossing you around when I become his wife?"

"No, not at all. I've heard we get time with the leftovers, if you know what I mean." He pushes me against the wall. "I want to hear you screaming in agony while I'm coming inside you,"

I push him away.

"Try it, and I'll have your balls as a necklace," I snarl.

He just laughs and pushes me into the sitting room.

"Jerk," I call back after him.

"Great, I have the rebel, Victoria, and here I was thinking that you might have learned something from the books I gave you."

Nicholas is sitting in the corner of the room, rubbing his forehead. He looks tired and in his hand is a glass of brandy. He lifts it to his lips and takes a long drink.

"Doesn't that burn your mouth?" I ask.

"No."

"Oh yeah. I forgot you're the devil so it probably seems cold to you."

"Can we cut the crap? You're the third woman I've spent time with today. Amelia gave me one-word answers to my questions, and Elizabeth spent most of it trying to suck my dick. Just be your natural self and not the argumentative bitch you portray. This is happening whether any of us like it or not, so let's make the best of it." He motions to the chair opposite him. "Please sit."

"You're not going to rape me?"

He laughs.

"That's what you thought would happen here?"

"Well, every time I've seen you so far, I've been manhandled and naked. It doesn't set a very high expectation." I raise an eyebrow at him while taking a seat. He slides me a glass of brandy across the table. I catch it, pick it up, and sniff it.

"It hasn't got drugs in it."

I take a little sip and am satisfied that I'm not being plied with Rohypnol.

"You'll have to forgive me for being skeptical."

"I'm not the monster you think I am."

"Am I free to go home then?"

"No." He takes a drink, and I copy. I lick my lips to take away the residue brandy on them.

"Then, I'm afraid, you're a monster and always will be. Real men don't need to kidnap and imprison women to choose a bride. They go out on dates, like normal people." I cross one of my legs over the other. He watches my thighs rub together in the tight fabric of the skinny jeans that I'm wearing.

"Which is why I asked you here."

"You think this counts as a date?" I snort a contemptuous laugh.

"It's the best I can offer. This isn't prescribed in the governing document. It's something I want to do, though."

"Impress us with your witty repertoire in the hope that one of us falls in love with your good looks and humor and agrees to marry you. I don't think that's going to happen. Not unless they're as insane as every man in this place."

He sits forward in his chair and brushes his hand through his hair. It's longer on the top than at the sides and ruffles down to leave him with a sexy bed head.

"You know, I thought the bravado was all an act, but

I'm beginning to see that you really are a bitch."

"I'm not a bitch. The situation has just made me a little angry," I interrupt and get to my feet ready to storm away.

"No, you're a spoiled little rich girl. I bet Daddy has always given you what you wanted all your life?" He gets to his feet and grabs my arm and turns me around to face him. I try to pull away, but he holds my arm tightly. "At least you've had twenty-one years of a normal life. I've known about having to force a woman to marry me almost since I was born. It was the first thing I learned, pretty much, before I could even talk. That kind of messes with a kid's head, knowing his life is mapped out for him, and there's nothing he can do about it."

I try to pull away again but can feel his strong grip tighten and dig into my slender arm.

"You think my life has been normal? It's been far from it. Maybe knowing about my future would have made my childhood more understandable," I respond and give up struggling. I lean further into him, so our faces are inches away from each other. I am so angry. "My childhood was spent in the company of a governess. I watched my brother and my only friend, a maid's daughter, go off to school and come home talking about all the friends they made. They would go to parties, the park, concerts. Every single time I asked to go, I was told 'no'. If I left the house, it was under my father's supervision. I dreamed of going to university, of getting away, having a life, and learning more about art. But my father's answer was always the same - that I didn't need to work, so what would be the point in me learning things like that? I spent day after day alone. I had no idea why, until I was brought here. You think that's a normal life? Then, you're a bigger fool than you look. You may have known you would become a monster, but

I had no idea I would become your victim."

He winces at my words. He lets me go and stumbles back into his chair. I should run away while I can, but my feet won't take me. Instead, I stay still, my chest heaving as I try to calm myself, after my fiery explosion.

"I went to university and studied Art. It was fun. What would your specialty have been?"

"My what?" My voice is quiet now.

"What would you have focused on? Fine arts? History of Art? Digital Arts?"

"History."

"I did digital. Art on computers. Why history?"

I look back at the chair, and he nods for me to sit.

"I like learning about paintings, the history behind them, and the artist who painted them. I like learning why they made certain strokes the way they did, and what it reflects about them in the painting."

"I've seen you looking at all the paintings around the house." He relaxes back into his chair and crosses his left ankle over his right leg. I sit forward in mine. I'm still anxious being here and want to be ready to run, should I need to.

"You have some good examples. Do they come from the Duke's work with the London galleries?"

"He's well connected when it comes to purchasing artwork. It helps him get the ones he wants."

I laugh — it's a sweet and genuine chuckle, which catches me by surprise. I've no idea where the sound comes from.

"What?" he asks curiously. He is intrigued to know what has triggered me to let my guard down around him.

"I was just thinking. I hope that those contacts didn't advise him to spend a lot of money on Van Gogh's Poppies. I doubt that's the original since it was stolen eight years ago in Egypt."

It’s his turn to laugh, this time. I feel as though it's a private joke he’s not ready to share with me.

“I don't know the price my father paid. It would serve him right if he had indeed been tricked. He’s too pretentious when it comes to art. He likes the finest and will often overlook pieces by more modern artists.”

“Modern artists are just as good as the Old Masters, in my mind. Is that why you chose digital to specialize in?” I’m slightly scared of the accord we have formed. I know my facts when it comes to art. For someone with no formal qualifications, I’m well read. Discussing masterpieces with someone is enjoyable.

“I learned a lot about fine arts and history from my father. I guess choosing digital art was my way of fighting against what he expected.”

“You and your father seem to do that a lot.”

“Can we get off the conversation of my father, please. It leaves a bitter taste in my mouth.” He shuts down the conversation with no room for me to continue it, in any way.

“Sorry.” I pick up my glass and drink the last mouthful of brandy. He holds the bottle up to offer more.

“No, thank you. My father never allowed me to drink a lot. It’s probably best I don’t have too much.”

“Did your father allow you to do anything?” he enquires with genuine interest.

“Not really. I had my friend, Tamara, my maid’s daughter. I was allowed out once to a restaurant with her. But I had to have a bodyguard with me, and even then, my father called us home before dessert when he found out that several male friends of Tamara’s had arrived at the place we were eating.” I pause and go silent. I’m trying to find a good memory of my father. Currently, they’re all tainted with the hate I now feel toward him. “He once allowed me to go to an art sale.

He brought a Van Gogh picture there. It was a wonderful experience, even if I did almost go into shock when he offered twenty million for the picture."

"Twenty million? That's a lot."

"Yes, you would think that he'd have it locked away never to see the light of day, but he displays in our dining room, sometimes." I laugh again, and he smiles at me. The conversation we're having is natural and not strained, but I still feel nervous because of the situation I'm in.

"I'll have all your art books returned, so you can read more about the history of paintings."

My good mood is sullied. He's just reminded me that I'm a slave here. I can do nothing that he, himself, doesn't allow. I sit a little more upright in my chair, and my manicured nails grip the seat.

"I'm to be here a long time, then?"

"A while longer."

"And then?"

"Depends on my choice."

"So my fate, my life, rests in your hands?" I purse my lips together, and I can feel the anger rising in me again.

"It does."

I shake my head.

"I don't get it. You tell me you don't want to marry, but yet you continue with this," –I hold my hands out– "whatever it is. Put a stop to it. Let us go."

He sighs heavily.

"I can't do that."

"Why not?"

"Because it's my fate, just as it's yours. It's my birthright, nothing will ever change that. Please, Victoria, just accept what's happening, and it'll all be much easier for you." He gets to his feet while speaking and holds his hand out to me. I look down at his hand as though it's severely infected with all manner of diseases. He actually expected me just to accept this.

"I see it, now. You're a coward. That's why you go along with this. You may be resigned to the legacy of your succession." –I get to my feet and push past him with surprising strength and head to the door– "I never will be, though. You and your father have started a war. One you won't win."

CHAPTER TWELVE

NICHOLAS

I shake the three-quarters empty decanter of brandy. I think I should stop drinking. Since Victoria left me alone with her stinging words, I've drunk another three glasses. I'm not inebriated, but I'm on the way. I need to keep my wits about me while my father's on his mission to have me married off and not in a way I care to.

It is getting late. I get to my feet and stretch my legs out. I must've been seated in the same chair for a couple of hours. I'm an energetic person, most of the time. I love to go to the gym, swim, play tennis, horse ride, and drive cars really fast. Sitting down reflecting on life isn't something that I do all that often, but I'm feeling lethargic and have no desire to exercise. Maybe reading for a bit will quieten my mind and send me to sleep. I stumble in the dark to the library. The great-grandfather clock strikes eleven at night. Damn, I really was sitting there for a long time. I run a finger over the shelves searching for something that captures my attention enough to read. Nothing. Most of these books I've read, at some point in time — the remainder are just too old and boring. I turn around to look at the other side of the room, and my gaze goes instantly to the antique chest of drawers that sits proudly by the heavily carved door at the entrance to the room. My chest tightens — I know it's time as I take slow steps closer, toward the unit. I pull open the drawer, containing my mother's diary, which she wrote after she was brought to Oakfield Hall for the first time. My father's arrogant enough to just leave it lying around. The information it contains, I've been told, is potentially destructive. But then, I'm sure my father would just claim madness as the reason for my mother's words. I pull the diary out and stroke the embroidered cover. It's covered in the most elegant silk and etched with a monochrome of her name, Katherine. I was five when she died. She was only a year older than I am now. I barely even remember her. I open the cover and turn to the first page.

"My life changed today. I don't know if it'll be for the better or worse yet. All I know is that it has changed.

I was brought to Oakfield Hall to be entered into a contest to become the wife of Henry Cavendish. My father had told me it would happen when I turned twenty-one, but that doesn't make it any easier, leaving everything I know behind. This place is full of men. I don't see any women except for six other terrified girls like myself. The current Duchess of Oakfield keeps to herself and looks so sad.

There's something malevolent lurking beneath the surface here as well. I was branded. That doesn't seem normal, but in this place I don't know what is right or wrong anymore."

I wince at the thought of my mother being permanently scarred in the same way as the girls. She was my mother and shouldn't have been treated that way. Now, I'm just being ridiculous. I come from a long line of women who were chosen in the same way. I flick through a few pages.

"We had a horrible task today. I can't even write about it. It broke me. I'm not that person. I don't do these things. Why have I been put in this position?"

I turn more pages, unable to read about the tasks my

mother had to endure.

"Henry Cavendish made his decision today. He chose me. The other girls were taken away, and I heard their screams most of the night as the other men in the society took turns with them. I feel so guilty. Why did he decide on me? I'm nothing special. We're to be married tomorrow. I don't think I've ever been so scared in my life. Henry isn't a nice man. He takes delight in what he's done to us. He isn't a man with humanity or kindness in his heart. God, give me strength. I never thought that this would be the life of a Duchess."

I slam the book shut and heave. My hands are shaking. Is this the type of man I am? Is this what Victoria, Elizabeth, and Amelia think of me? I turn and walk away from the diary. I can't read anymore. I have to do this — I don't have a choice. A few more weeks and this part will be over. I force an exasperated breath from my lips. One more passage, I tell myself. One more passage. Going back to my mother's journal, I open a page toward the end.

"They took my son from me today. My husband blames me for him not being perfect, but in my eyes he's everything. I have nothing left. This will be my last entry. I can't do it anymore. He'll come to me tonight and beat me black and blue. He'll force himself on me, and my body will die just as my mind did all those years ago. Goodbye, Katherine Cavendish, Duchess of Oakfield."

There are no further entries in the diary. I look at the date written at the top of the page, but I already know in my heart what it will be. It's the date of my mother's death. I close the book again and put it back in the drawer. One day, when this is all over, I'll read it again, but now her words will weaken me, and I can't allow that to happen. I need to be strong to be the man that my father wants me to be. Maybe, when I'm Duke, I can work on changing the rules, but for the time being, there's nothing that can be done. Victoria Hamilton may think that I'm a coward, but she doesn't understand anything. She's lived in a bubble, not the real world. It's do or die out there, and I have no plans on dying just yet.

My mother's words haunt me though,

"They took my son from me."

I wish she were talking about me in that statement, but she isn't. No, I have a brother. I've never understood why people call him *wrong*. He's just William to me. I think he's just what I need. I stumble down the corridor, again in the dark, toward his room. It's as far away from my father's as possible. The Duke has nothing to do with William, unless it's vital. I unlock the door and enter without knocking. I know he'll be awake. He likes to watch the stars.

"Hi, Bro." I swagger in and hold my arms open.

"Out!" he shouts back from his vantage point next to his telescope at the window.

"Why?" I ask in confusion.

"You didn't knock." He frowns.

"Do I really need to do that?"

He flicks his hand across his head, around his nose, and taps his foot twice. I can see he's getting agitated. William was diagnosed as being on the autism spectrum at a young age. In fact, the day my mother died. Most people think of a person with autism as having social inadequacies and learning disabilities, but William's nothing like that. He's incredibly intelligent, far superior to me. He has his quirks — like the fact, he's looking at me as though I've grown three heads because I didn't knock on his door before entering. But other than that, he's perfectly normal. Any social inadequacies are more likely to come from the fact that, since his diagnosis, my father has hidden him away in this room with only a governess for company most of the time. I think that would make it hard for anyone to interact the way that society decrees.

"I'm sorry." I hold my hands up and step back toward the door. "I'll come in again."

"Three knocks." His brows furrow together in anguish.

"Three knocks. I promise."

I leave the room again and shut the door. This time before entering I knock three times and open. William's smiling this time, and the anxiety of before is gone. Such a simple thing can agitate him so much. I feel guilty for upsetting him.

"Sorry," I offer.

"It's ok. His Grace came here earlier, and he always refuses to knock. I was scared it was him again."

"What did he want?" I hate the thought of my father upsetting William. He's two years younger than me, and I care a great deal for him.

"To tell me to make sure I'm quiet while we have guests. He doesn't want them finding out about me. I embarrass him." William sits down on a sofa. "I think Bertha told him I was playing my guitar earlier."

I sit next to him and place my arm around him.

"If you want to play your guitar, then play it. You're good at it. You could be in a band. Ignore Bertha and the Duke. They've got no taste." Bertha is my brother's governess. He doesn't need her — he's twenty-six for god's sake, but my father insists. She's William's jailer. The first thing I'll do when I'm Duke is get rid of her and allow William to see the world. He's been cooped up in this house since he was three. I hate it.

“I shouldn’t. The girls may hear me.”

“They’re my girls, not father’s. I’m not ashamed of you like he is.”

William looks down at his hands. He taps one, his left on his leg three times and then the right three times. His autism is focused very much around routine. It comforts him.

“I’m not, William, I promise. When I’m Duke, everything will change. Father will leave for the country, and we can rule together. Brothers side by side.”

“What about your wife?” he asks.

I go quiet.

“This doesn’t have to be your legacy, you know.” William offers with optimism in his voice. “Your succession could be different.”

“Not you as well. It can’t — I have to go through with this.”

“Not necessarily.”

“To try to end this madness would assign far too many people to death. You and the girls downstairs included.

I kick my shoes off and push back on his sofa, my head resting on the duck down cushion.

“I may not be seen, Nicholas, but I do a lot of seeing. She’s strong enough.”

What?” I rub my hands over my eyes. Now that I’ve laid my head down, my eyes are tired. The alcohol and the emotions are draining the strength from me.

“I may not remember Mother, but she was weak. Victoria isn’t”

“What has Victoria got to do with this?” My eyes drift shut. I’m trying to listen to him, but it’s becoming a struggle. William has always been a comfort blanket to me. We’ve snuck into each other's room since we were little. Thankfully, Bertha and our father only caught us a few times.

"You have goodness in you. You aren't the devil Father wants you to portray."

I yawn.

"I think you're deliberately trying to confuse me. With all that 'seeing' you're doing, you must know I've drunk a lot of brandy."

I fall asleep to William laughing at me.

CHAPTER THIRTEEN

VICTORIA

"Tell me what you want me to do to you, Victoria?" Nicholas stands before me. He's naked, but I can't make out the lower half of his body. It's hazy. That seems so strange.

"I can't," I whisper back.

"Do you want me to touch you here?"

He touches my breasts, and I let out a moan.

"Maybe here."

He dips his finger into my mouth, and I wrap my tongue around it.

"No. Definitely here." I feel my pussy start to throb.

"Please," I whimper. "More."

"You like that." That arrogant grin crosses his lips. I want to smack him in his face, but he touches me down there again, and I buck off the bed.

"Fuck!" I squirm under his touch. "Take me. Make me yours."

"Who am I to disappoint, my little Duchess?"

CRASH!

I sit bolt upright in my bed. My breathing is fast, and the ache between my legs has my hand fly there to touch myself in the hope of relief. It's then I notice the human-shaped shadow moving in my room.

"Nicholas?" I pray it's no one else. The person's physique is the same stature as my captor. "Is that you?"

"Sorry." A deep voice rumbles. Then the intruder

pulls at something by the wall, which reveals a secret door through which he disappears. I rub my eyes. Was I dreaming *that* as well as Nicholas about to take my virginity? My hand is still between my thighs, and I'm wet there. That part was a dream. I think I'm going to suppress the dream because otherwise it will freak me out. The more pressing matter is the man who was in my room and where he's gone? I turn my bedside lamp on and swing my legs out of the bed. I put on slippers and pull a lightweight robe over my shoulders. It's summer, but there's a little chill in the air tonight. There always seems to be in these big houses. Nothing looks out of the norm in my bedroom. Well, except for the mirror that I stare into daily, wondering how this has become my life. It's slightly ajar from the wall. I pull it, and a doorway opens. A secret passageway. My heart flutters with excitement. Maybe, this is a way out. The person, whoever he was, was showing me how to escape. I look around for anything I can use to light my way. I'd do anything to be back in my bedroom at home, right now. I have a love of candles. Then again, I wouldn't need this secret tunnel if I were at home. I can't waste any more time and decide that I'll just have to enter it in the dark. I pick a couple of books up and wedge them against the door, to keep it open and offer a little light. Especially when I turn on the overhead light in my room to add illumination. I peek inside the doorway. Spider webs are everywhere. My stomach churns. I'm such a wimp when it comes to those little creatures with eight legs. Big girl pants time, spiders can do a lot less damage to me now than the other occupants of Oakfield Hall. I step inside the dark stone corridor. Oakfield Hall is a brick mansion, and this hidden chamber must have been built within the walls. I chuckle as I imagine the clandestine liaisons that they may have been used for in the past. I look to my left, and it's boarded up, so I can't go that way. Right it is. My heart is beating so fast I'm sure that I can hear it vibrating off the walls. I hear a noise up ahead and quicken my pace a little. There is no light. I'm terrified, especially when I bump into some stairs and only just manage to keep my footing. I bend low to the floor and trace them up in a crouching position. I have no idea what I'm touching, and I really don't want to know. I get to the top of the steps and look around. It's still pitch black. Surely, to get out of this place I would need to go down, not up. I'm not going to take any chances with my footing again, for fear of tumbling downstairs, I keep low and crawl along the floor. Up ahead, I see a flicker of light. Is this where the person who was in my room has gone? Maybe they're waiting to free me? I scamper forward quickly, on all fours, then stop and listen at the doorway where the light is.

"Silly, silly. You shouldn't have left the room." I hear from the other side.

I push the door slowly. It creaks open and sitting there is a man. I recognize his features, instantly. They're the same as the ones I was just dreaming of, but younger and paler. Nicholas must have a brother.

The man swipes his hand across his head, around his nose, and taps the floor twice with his foot.

"Hello," I say quietly.

He looks up at me with fear in his eyes.

"You can't be here."

"You were in my room?"

"Yes." He does his strange movement again. It seems to be some sort of tic.

"Why? Who are you?"

"You must go back." He scrambles a little farther away.

"I won't hurt you. I just want to know who you are?"

I slide my body out of the secret passageway and step into the room. It's opulently decorated like a sitting room. A television sits in the corner with a games console attached to it, and a table is laid ready for breakfast. I went upstairs in the tunnel — I must've come to the second floor. There's a door to the other end of the room, and I wonder where that leads.

"You have to knock before you come in."

"Knock?" I enquire in confusion.

"Please, do it four times."

The man's strange behavior is getting worse. The agitation in his stance flooding the room with more fear than I have. I don't know why, but I go back to the doorway and knock four times.

"Come in," he calls quietly. "Thank you." He places both his hands down on his thighs and starts to tap a two beat on each leg alternately.

"Hello, I'm Victoria."

"I know. I've read your file." He leans over to the side and picks up a wrapped gift. "I was bringing you this, but you moved the chair. I crashed into it and knocked the vase over. You shouldn't move furniture. It makes it more difficult to understand."

"I'm sorry." I find myself apologizing again. "I'll put it all back. Can I ask who you are?"

"I'm William, Nicholas' brother." He doesn't meet my gaze but hands me the present. "Open it."

"I..." I'm lost for words. "You didn't have to get me this."

"I want you to like me — when you become Duchess."

His blunt verbiage is surprising in this house of lies.

"I don't think I'll become Duchess but thank you anyway."

"You should have more faith in yourself." He waves the gift insistently in front of me. I take it and unwrap it. It's a book on art.

"You didn't have to get me this." I reach forward and

try to touch his hand in thanks, but he pulls it away.

"I've seen you read all the other books. This is the third one in the collection about Rembrandt. You spent a lot of time on those books."

"You've been watching me?" I shuffle farther away from him. I don't like the fact that he's been invading my private space.

"We can watch all the girls via the screens." He nods toward his TV. I must pale or look like I'm going to throw up, which I certainly feel could happen, because he gasps. "That's one of those things that I'm not supposed to say out loud, isn't it?"

"It's a little scary to know that people are watching me." I raise my eyebrows. "Why aren't you supposed to say it out loud?"

"I have autism. I often say things I shouldn't. I can't help it. When I first saw you on the screen, I told Nicholas that you had the best tits I've ever seen."

I must blush because he groans.

"See. I really can't help it."

"That's ok — it's nice to be appreciated." I laugh and this seems to relax William, a little, as he settles down. "Why haven't you been with your brother and father when they've been...um?"

"Torturing you?" he offers.

"Pretty much."

"My father doesn't allow me out with his society. He's embarrassed by me. I'm the reason my mother died, because I was wrong. It's better if I just hide out up here."

"That isn't right. I'm sorry."

"It's alright. I'm used to it. Safer to be in these four walls than out there." He looks toward the door — a means of escape. I take a sharp inhalation of breath. This could be my chance.

"You don't want to go through there." He taps my

leg.

"Why?"

As if by magic, the door opens and a sleepy looking Nicholas stands in the opening.

"What the fuck!" He exclaims and stomps toward me. "What the hell are you doing in here?" He grabs me and pulls me to my feet like I'm a rag doll.

"Get off me," I shout and attempt to kick out. I just miss his leg.

"Nick, it was my fault. Please don't hurt her."

Nicholas looks toward the door that I entered the room through.

"You're an idiot. Damn it." Nicholas' grip on me becomes even tighter and drags me back to the hole in the wall. "Get to bed, William. If our father asks about this, you haven't left your room all evening. You hear me?"

"Yes." William holds the book up for me. "I just wanted to give this to her."

"Not now. I'll come back and get it later." Nicholas pushes me back through the door and starts to shove me through the dark corridor. I remember there are stairs somewhere around here, and just as I'm about to tumble down them, Nicholas grabs me. He slams me against the wall. I can't see him, but I can feel the anger emanating from him.

"If anything happens to William because you were in that room, then I'll kill you with my bare hands."

CHAPTER FOURTEEN

NICHOLAS

The need to protect herself must suddenly occur to Victoria because before I realize what she intends to do, she raises her leg and thrusts it hard into my shin. I step back and grab my aching leg.

"Bitch," I growl, but she doesn't hear me because she's taken off fast down the corridor. She manages the steps down without any trouble, and I listen to her rapid breathing in the darkness. I chase after her with murderous intent. William is my flesh and blood — he's my closest ally in this house, and I won't see any harm come to him from anyone. Especially a stuck up girl who thinks that she's better than her allotted place in life. She thinks I'm a coward. I'll show her just what I can do. She reaches her room and kicks at a pile of books holding the door open and tries to shut it. She's too late and too weak against my superior strength. I push the door open and stalk into her room. The lights are already on, and I can see that she's like a frightened little rabbit, cowering backward into a corner.

"Big mistake," I sneer.

"He came to me first," she pleads.

"William doesn't understand what he's doing. He thinks he's nice, but he doesn't understand the trouble it'll get him into with my father. You should have sent him away and certainly shouldn't have followed him." I prowl closer to her, closing the distance between us like a cheetah ready to pounce.

"You forget something. I'm not the monster in this

house. I'm just as much of a victim as it seems your brother is. Both of us not allowed to leave and kept hidden away against our free will. If you want to look at who might hurt your brother, go look in a mirror," she hisses back at me. "Your brother was just being nice and bringing me a present."

I groan. Setting William up with an Amazon Prime account was the worst thing I'd ever done. I thought it would help alleviate the boredom he felt, but after he spent five thousand pounds on games consoles, books, and a massive television in the first month alone, I decided to limit his spending. He's obviously been on it again and buying presents for people that he really shouldn't.

"You have to promise me you won't tell anyone you saw him." She's in the corner, and I place both my hands on the wall either side of her. She's trapped. The only way out is to kick me again, but I'm anticipating that.

"Why?" she asks with utter contempt for me.

"Please?"

"Let me go, and I won't say a word. Let me walk out of this house, right now."

"You know I can't do that," I reply, sick of the same argument. Doesn't she realize that I could squash her like a fly?

"Why not?"

"For god's sake, Victoria. Just accept that this is happening. You aren't getting out of here anytime soon," I snap.

"Tell me something — I know what happens if you choose me. I get to be the Duchess of Oakfield and put my own children through the heartbreak I'm experiencing. What happens if you don't choose me?"

"I'm not talking about this. Just answer me. Will you keep quiet about William?"

"No, you answer me." She stamps her foot. I brace

myself just in case she's about to kick out again.

"God, you're the most infuriating woman I've ever known. Fine, you want to know what happens. If you survive the task, *if* being the poignant factor, and you lose, then you'll be taken by the other men and raped. You'll then be executed —since you'll know far too much. Face it. One way or another, your life's over. Accept it. Save my brother in the process. Don't drag him down with you."

She gasps, and her legs give way. She sinks to the floor at my feet.

"How can you do this to me? You don't even know me. How can you be so cruel?" Tears pool in her eyes, but they don't fall. Despite her moment of weakness, she won't allow me the indignity of seeing her cry.

"It's not personal. If I could change things, then I would. I want this as much as you do." The anger of moments ago dissipates between us. I crouch down on the balls of my feet in front of her. "I've told you I have no choice. It's the only way to get rid of him."

"Your father?"

I nod an affirmative.

"I don't want to die."

"I don't want you to die. I don't want Elizabeth and Amelia to die either, but I have to get rid of him. Once I'm Duke, William can be seen. I'll be in charge. I'll make the rules."

"Will you change the rules of the society so that this doesn't happen to other people?"

I swallow deeply.

"I'll do what I can."

"You mean no." She pushes to her feet and walks past me to the bed. I follow her and wrap my arms around her. I don't know why. It just seems the right thing to do. She's distressed. She's been told she could die within the year.

“I don’t know if that’s a battle too far for me. I won’t ever stop trying, though.” I lay my head on her shoulder and whisper my words into her ear.

“William’s safe. I won’t mention I’ve seen him. He told me about the cameras you have on us. You might want to get rid of any video that’s been recorded.” She sounds defeated.

“Thank you. I’ll choose you in return if I can. I’ll make you the Duchess.”

She spins in my arms and faces me. The tears she’s been holding in begin to fall. Her stunning emerald eyes meet mine, and there's sadness and defeat in them.

“No, don’t make a promise you can’t keep. I’m not protecting William so I can gain favor with you. I’m doing it because he’s as much a victim of this house as I am.” She looks down at the ground. “I think it would be better if you go.” With a wriggle, she attempts to pull out of my arms. I grip tighter. I don’t want to go. She looks back up at me. “Earl Lullington, please.”

I bow my head and bring my lips down on hers. She’s soft and tastes of strawberries. At first, she doesn’t respond. I pull back and see that tears still fall. She opens and closes her mouth like she wants to tell me off, to shout, scream, and rant at me, but nothing comes out. I let go of her waist with one hand and use my fingers to wipe away her tears. She turns her head and kisses the tears from my digits. My breath hitches, and I lean back in to kiss her again. This time, she responds, and before I know it, we’re bumping into the bed and falling on top of it.

She breaks the kiss and stares at me intently.

“Make me feel. If I’m to die, allow me this one thing.”

I slide down her body. She’s wearing the silk dressing gown and set of pajamas that I bought for all the girls. Tradition dictates that they should wear these horrendous Victorian nightdress things, but I’m afraid they did nothing for me. If I can't see a woman naked, then I prefer her to look casual in low slung trousers and a tight t-shirt. I pull her pajama bottoms down and throw them on the floor. My face is inches from her pussy, and I can smell her arousal. It leaves a glistening coat on her neatly trimmed cleft. I shove my face in between her legs and start to sample her delights — like a man on death row consuming his last meal. I've eaten enough pussy to know a good one when I taste it, and this is the best ever. She's succulent, sweet and wet, just for me.

"That feels amazing." She squirms with pleasure under my exploration of her folds.

I pull my head up. "Has anyone ever given you oral sex before?"

She lifts her head up and raises an annoyed eyebrow at me.

"Err. You're the only man I've ever been alone with, except my father and brother. I don't know what other freaky things your family gets up to, but mine doesn't go for incest."

I chuckle and let it reverberate around her inner thighs. Even with my head in between her legs, she's still lippy. I like it.

"Believe me, neither my father or brother have attributes akin to yours, which entertain me in the slightest. I like the fact that I'm the first man to go down on you. I know once you've had me you won't want anyone else."

"Arrogant or what?" she snorts.

"It's my middle name."

I flex my index finger and tenderly sink it inside her. She clenches down on the intrusion — fuck, this is only a finger. I imagine sticking my cock inside her. She would grip me like a vice and milk the cum from my body in a violent explosion. But I mustn't get ahead of myself. First, I'm going to give her, her first orgasm from being licked out.

I push another finger inside her, and she groans even louder.

"So full."

"Wait until it's my cock."

I feel her entire body shiver under me. Dipping my head again, I devour her. It isn't long before she starts to writhe and jerk on the bed in a climatic orgasm. She moans my name in a raspy breath.

"Nicholas."

The way she says my name catches my breath and halts me in my exploits to send her high again. Fuck, what am I doing? I can't do this. I can't take her in this way. I can't develop feelings for her. It'll ruin everything. I jump from the bed. She sits up, her hair crazy with that 'just come' look.

"What's wrong?" she asks with disappointment on her face. "Did I do something wrong?"

"I'm not the man who should make you feel. I'm the devil. You've called me that yourself." I readjust my trousers, my cock is rock hard, and go to the door.

"What?" She slides from the bed on wobbly feet. Thankfully, her dressing gown covers her nakedness from me.

"Thank you for agreeing not to out William for his indiscretion. I'll see to it that he doesn't bother you again. You should get some sleep. We have a task tomorrow, and, as you've asked me not to, I won't go easy on you."

Her lips purse together, and her brow furrows. I know that she's about to hit me with another outburst, but I don't wait to hear it. I leave the room and take the steps to mine, two at a time. I can't get to it fast enough. The house is still dark apart from a small slither of moonlight cascading through the windows not covered by curtains. On entering my room, I slam and lock the door behind me. I need to relieve the ache in my pants. Fuck, I would have taken her there and then if my brain hadn't kicked in. I'm not here to fall in love with these girls. They're a means to an end: stick a child in them, raise the next generation, and free William from the confines of his seclusion imposed by my father. I drop my trousers and pump hard at my cock. I fist it so fast that I come in an instant. My essence spills onto the floor, but I don't care. I needed this release. I need to prove to her that I'm the devil who takes for himself. She's a lamb to the slaughter — a means to an end. I won't rest until I'm the next Duke of Oakfield.

CHAPTER FIFTEEN

VICTORIA

I'm naked underneath a gown again. I've learned enough to know, that doesn't end well. Elizabeth, Amelia, and I stand in front of the members of the society. The Duke and Nicholas are at the head of the group. They both wear tailored dark suits, white shirts, and matching ties. Nicholas fiddles with his ever-present cufflinks. He hasn't looked at me once since he entered the room. It's like he's brought a shutter down on what happened between us last night. I should step forward and shout at the Duke that William came into my room last night. I'm angry enough to do it because Nicholas is so damn stubborn. If only he would end what's going on, then we could all leave. He won't, though. His father controls him like a puppet on a string, and that's the reason why I won't tell on William. Feeling an intensity wash over me, I look toward Nicholas, his eyes are everywhere except on me. William, I look up at a balcony toward the top of the high ceiling. I can't see him although I know that he's there. He hides in the shadows. I can't help but envy him. I wish I were up there hiding with him. I look back down and toward Nicholas, and he's scowling at me. It's a warning — he must've seen me looking up. I shut my eyes and let out a long breath before mouthing,

"I promise."

I don't look at him again, for the Duke starts his speech that will lead to today's torture.

"Welcome again, gentlemen. I trust you all slept well.

It's been a few days since we conducted the last trial, and I'm sure you're all as excited as I am to continue with choosing a wife for my son." A few of the men murmur their eagerness to continue. I want to scream that they're all freaks, but I know it's better to hold my tongue. I shuffle my bare feet against the cold of the stone floor and wait to hear my fate.

"As the wife of a Duke, the chosen woman will need to take discipline and thank her husband for it. She'll be expected to be impeccably behaved and subservient to his needs at all times, but by nature, they're women and thus prone to faults. This task looks at how well the women before us will take the discipline that Nicholas will give to them, and it will probably set a precedent for the future of their marriage." The Duke laughs. I find myself beyond caring at this point. I thought I was getting somewhere with Nicholas, last night, but when he pulled away, it all crumbled, and I was the one who realized that my fate and his are intertwined forever. Until he understands the hold that his father has over him and stops lying to himself, there's nothing I can do to save either of us.

"Ladies. Would you remove your cloaks and form a line in front of Nicholas? He'll ask you a question, and you should answer it as you feel he would want you to."

I can't help but think that sounds a little too simple for a task. Where's the humiliation? I suddenly fear the question he'll ask. I remove my gown, as do Elizabeth and Amelia, and we stand as ordered. Nicholas walks the line. He stops in front of each of us and looks us up and down. I notice no interest on his face with Elizabeth and Amelia, but when it comes to me, the way he looks between my legs has me rub them together at the memory of his head in between my thighs. His nostrils flare as though he's aware of the arousal pooling between my legs. Fuck. I can't get horny for this monster. I'll become the freak then. I look down at the floor, and he walks back to Elizabeth.

"Miss Sandford, if we're out at a social function, and I ask you to get on your hands and knees, bark like a dog, and crawl around the room, would you?" Some of the assembled crowd laugh at his question, but it just confirms to me how insane this is.

Elizabeth pulls on a strand of her jet black hair and pouts at the question. She's pretending to mull it over? I can see the look on her face. I really haven't warmed to this girl. She seems to actually be enjoying what's going on. I, on the other hand, want to just gag. When she gets to her knees and barks like a dog, I'm pretty confident that I'm going to be sick.

"I'll do whatever you ask of me. As my husband, you'll be my master, and I'll obey your every command because you need to be satisfied in all things."

Yep, definitely feeling queasy.

"Thank you, Elizabeth." Nicholas smiles at her and offers his hand to allow her to get back on her feet. He kisses it and moves onto Amelia. The blonde haired girl seems to be stronger today. She's been dealing with the situation the worst of all of us. I've been desperate to get to know her better — I might be able to help support her, but we haven't had the opportunity to talk amongst ourselves. She turns her head to look at me and smiles with reassurance.

"Keep your eyes on me, Miss Rushbrooke, not Miss Hamilton."

"Apologies, Lord Lullington," she whispers, and I see her hands start to shake. Even though he isn't looking at me, I frown at Nicholas with utter scorn. He doesn't need to be such an obnoxious bully.

"The same question. What's your answer?"

"Yes, I would, My Lord." She doesn't hesitate in her answer, but there's no feeling in the words. They're said only because she needs to give an answer, and that's the one she thinks Nicholas wants to hear.

"Thank you, Amelia," Nicholas replies and comes to stand in front of me. He keeps his stare focused on my face, and I'm glad for that. The last thing I need is to have my thoughts muddled by lust.

"Miss Hamilton, what's your answer to the same question?" My survival instincts tell me to say yes and be done with it. Move on to the next task without torture, but the passion that burns inside me screams for me to tell him to go to hell. I find my own hands shaking. My legs feel like jelly. I just want to run and hide from the question. Why is it so difficult to answer? I swallow deeply and press my hands to my side to calm the tremor in them.

"Yes..." – I pause. Nicholas smiles– "should be my answer, but my father raised me not to tell lies. If I said yes and forego any punishment you are about to give me, then it would be deceitful to the *truth* of this situation." My last point's a sarcastic dig at what happened between Nicholas and me last night. He knows this is wrong but won't do anything about it. "My answer is, no, Earl Lullington. I wouldn't get to my knees and be a dog if you asked me to. Because you keep me here against my free will, you don't deserve my respect enough to do what you ask of me."

Nicholas' face reddens, and a vein in the side of his neck pulses furiously. Its beat matches that of the thundering tempo of my heart. He doesn't speak, though. He turns away from me and faces his father.

"Elizabeth Sandford was the most honest. She won't be punished as she doesn't need it. Amelia Rushbrooke, though she answered 'yes', I feel would be hesitant in obeying the order. Therefore, she'll be locked in her room for twenty-four hours with no food." He pauses, and my heart leaps into my mouth. "Victoria Hamilton was insolent and rude. She wouldn't obey my order and will get a harsh correction. She'll be whipped, here and now, twenty times. That would be my right as her husband."

I can barely take in his words. I expected a punishment but this? Whipping? It's cruel and degrading, not to mention will leave me scarred for life and in so much pain. Is this the sort of man Nicholas truly is? I was a fool to believe he might have kindness in him. He's lost — lost to the devil that is his father. I'm going to die. I'm twenty-one years old, a baby, and my life's over.

CHAPTER SIXTEEN

NICHOLAS

My shoulders slump in defeat, but the anger in me bubbles below the surface. I don't want to do this to Victoria, but she's forcing my hand. Why does she have to be so stubborn? I've told her just to comply with the rules, and I'll choose her as my wife. I'll save her life. What happens now is her fault, not mine. I have to do these punishments — they're prescribed in the founding documentation. She could be going to her room to rest and read her books, like Elizabeth and Amelia are, but no, she had to open her mouth again and spout a load of abuse. I'm not a liar. This is my right, to have a wife chosen for me this way. She should obey me.

I hold my right hand out, and a birch is placed in it. The bunch of thick twigs is the weapon of choice of the upper classes. In eighteenth-century schools, it was used to punish naughty boys. Girl's didn't attend schools. Their duty was to learn how to be a wife. I remember when I was eight years old my father took a birch to me. This particular one is handed down through the generations of our family. I can't remember exactly what I'd done, but it was something silly–like refusing to eat my dinner of brussel sprouts. Needless to say after getting hit a few times, I have eaten the rotten vegetable ever since. I've experienced what Victoria's about to receive. I was only hit a few times, though. She'll be left broken and bruised, after twenty hard hits. I can't temper my aim or strength with everyone watching. My father will know that I've gone easy on her and use it against me.

He'll demand blood, and he'll want to hear screaming. Blood, sweat, and tears, a misinterpretation of the saying, are the things he likes to witness coming from a woman the most.

Two of my father's assistants step forward and grab both of Victoria's arms. She's shocked and tries to struggle against them, but they're too strong for her. She's ushered, reluctantly, forward on the tips of her toes and bent over a table. The position leaves her pussy exposed for everyone to see. I step in front of her to block the view from the rest of the assembled society members. I don't want anyone else seeing her that way.

"I'd keep as still as you can. I can't guarantee my aim if you're moving around." I offer her advice in a helpful whisper.

"Fuck you," is her response. It angers me even more, and I bring the birch up and strike down on her pert bottom. She screams, and the flesh reddens.

"One." I count and raise my arm ready to strike her again.

"Stop." My father's voice fills the cavernous room.

"Your Grace." I turn and face him.

"I've just remembered something." The malevolent grin, which fills his face, has me shudder in anticipation. I'm glad that Victoria can't see him. "There aren't three punishments on the binding documentation. There are four." He strides confidently over to a box in the corner of the room. "The fourth has only been used once before on my grandmother. She was insolent and rude up until that point, but after this punishment, she became the perfect broken wife."

The men either side of Victoria let go of her — she stands up and rubs her bottom where I've just hit her with the birch. She turns and scowls at me. I return the look of contempt with all the anger still boiling inside of me and re-focus my attention on my father. He opens the box and pulls out an iron mask.

"Fuck," I exclaim, when I realize what he holds, and drop the birch. Victoria presses closer to me.

"What is it?" she asks with a tremble in her voice.

"A scold's bridle." I gulp the same time as my stomach clenches in disbelief.

"My grandmother was placed in this and humiliated in front of the society. She was beaten and berated with no method of response that wouldn't cut her tongue." My father steps forward holding the bridle. He's deliberately malicious.

"I've already chosen her punishment." I push Victoria aside and stand up to him.

"It's too tame for this heathen." My father grits his teeth together as he speaks. He shoves the bridle into my hands. It's heavy and the ironwork rusted from its age. "Put it on her."

"No. I chose the twenty lashes."

"The Duchess of Oakfield needs to be subservient. Twenty lashes won't cure Victoria Hamilton of her tongue — only humiliation will. You put her in this position, do it, or are you too weak to warrant the title of the Duke of Oakfield?" he sneers, and I want to punch him on his self-righteous chin. He knows full well that I'll submit to what he orders of me. I want the position to get rid of him, to provide a better life for William. I'm changing, and the man I was a few days ago is dying.

The bridle weighs heavy in my hands. I look down at it. The hinged iron framework encloses the head, and a bit fits into the mouth to suppress the tongue. Many have a smooth bit, but this one has a metal spike on it. If Victoria tries to speak while wearing it, the spike will rip into her tongue.

"Put. It. On. Her." My father's words are slow and menacing.

I'm wavering and want to run.

I feel the warmth of another hand over mine. It's Victoria's. She steps in front of me and takes the bridle. She places it over her own head and takes the bit into her mouth. She gags and whimpers when the spike must hit her tongue. She bows her head, so that I can fasten the contraption up.

"Excellent." My father steps forward clapping. "Maybe, the little bitch finally realizes that the word of man is law."

"The word of man is all lies," I comment quietly, and Victoria's eyes flash up to mine in understanding.

A clinking of metal has me flick my head around quickly. My father holds a chain.

"Time to walk your dog, my son."

He hands me the chain, and without looking at Victoria again, I attach it to her collar. This torture's all about humiliation for the victim. In olden times, the woman was walked around the village and abuse was actively encouraged, sexual and physical. She was called a variety of degrading names and left without food or water for hours. She was humiliated in every way, shape, or form for gossiping or talking back. Men sometimes suffered the same fate, but this was primarily a punishment for women.

"Gentlemen. In the box, there are horse whips. All marks must be confined to her back. You aren't to touch her sexually. Call her as many names as you wish, while Earl Lullington walks her in front of you. This woman has too much spirit, and, as you're all married, I'm sure you'll understand how harmful that can be to a man. It needs to be broken. Nicholas, proceed."

My feet feel like lead weights as I take the chain in my hand and step one foot in front of the other. I can't turn around and look at the pain being inflicted on Victoria. I'm a coward and not ashamed to admit it. The taunts she's receiving are enough for me.

"Whore."

"Bitch."

"Cock tease."

"Cunt."

"Slut."

"Virago."

I wince at every word, and the comments are even worse.

"Learn your place."

"On your knees and worship my feet."

"Cut her tongue out if she doesn't stop."

"Only good for fucking."

"Stick your dick in her mouth to shut her up."

"Women need to learn silence."

I make three passes. My father tells me to go for a fourth, but I feel the chain go taut over my shoulder. I turn around, and Victoria has slumped down onto the floor. I let it go and check on her. She's unconscious — her back bleeding and raw. One of the men steps forward with his whip held high.

"Enough," I snap.

He inclines his head in a bow and returns to the line.

"You, and you." I point to two of the guards. "Get this thing off her and return her to her room. Touch her intimately, while she's naked, and I'll use that sword" –I point to a massive metal blade hanging ominously on the wall– "to personally remove your hands."

They scramble to attention, and Victoria's limp body is removed from the room. I make a mental note that, as soon as I leave here, I'll have my personal doctor called to tend to her wounds, not the horrendous Dr. Fredrick Fallen. The other members of the society head to the bar to pour themselves a congratulatory round of brandies.

"Happy?" I face down my father who's picked up the bridle and is running his finger over the bit. Blood coats his digit where it must've dug into Victoria's tongue.

"Indeed. Although, it's yet to be seen whether she's actually learned her lesson or not. If you make her Duchess the way she currently is, it'll be the downfall of this family."

I laugh. I can't help it. I don't know where it comes from. It's probably the most natural reaction that I've ever had in my life.

"Or she might just be the savior of it."

I don't wait to hear his answer because my feet are propelling me toward the door and the woman I fear I've just destroyed.

CHAPTER SEVENTEEN

VICTORIA

I don't want to open my eyes. Am I dead? No, surely I wouldn't be in this much pain if I were. I try to shift on the bed from my front to my back but freeze the second that I experience a ricochet of agony so blinding, it shoots through my body. I cry out. I can't help it, which aggravates the wound on my tongue. The metallic taste of blood fills my mouth — I've opened a laceration.

"Wait, I'll help you" –a gentle feminine voice offers – "you're still very bruised."

"Amelia?" I recognize her soft tones at once.

"Yes," she replies, and I feel the cover's being shifted from my back. "Do you want to sit up?"

"Please," I respond, and she helps me to turn over and sit. She places a soft cushion under my bottom despite the fact that I'm on my bed. I feel sick from the pain, and it makes my head spin. "What happened?" My mind feels foggy. I have a vague recollection of a mask and name calling.

I retch. The names were so cruel. Amelia puts a small bowl in front of me, and I dry heave over it. Every jolt of my body sends aches through me. I have nothing to bring up as I haven't eaten or drunk for what seems like ages. I look down at my hand and see a cannula in it. I look up at Amelia and try to speak, but I'm breaking down.

"Breathe. It's alright. You're safe." She touches my hand. "Do you remember the punishment they gave you?"

I look into the haze that is my brain and remember the scold's bridle and the horsewhips. I blank the name calling. I'm not going to remember that again.

"Yes, they whipped me."

She nods.

"You were in bad shape. We thought you may die. The Earl called for his doctor. You have some deep wounds, which were stitched up. They gave you morphine to help with the pain and fluid to keep you hydrated. That's why you have this." She looks at the device in my hand. "It was thought best to let you sleep for a few days to allow your body to start healing. They stopped all the drugs this morning. I have some extra strength painkillers here if you need them." This time, she holds up a bottle.

"Yes, please." I don't hesitate. Give me all the drugs you can to numb the agony in my body. The morphine drip sounds good. Maybe I could get hooked back up on that.

Amelia hands me two pills and helps me sit forward to drink some water. My throat is raw, and the water mixes with the blood in my mouth. It's not a pleasant experience.

"They've advised you not to talk too much. The bridle had a spike on it, and when you passed out, it cut your tongue. It was rusty due to its age, and they feared you may lose your tongue to infection, but it seems alright. You need to rest it to let it heal." I take her advice and nod my response rather than speak it.

I collapse my head back against the headboard of the bed, I'm grateful for the plethora of cushions that cocoon me. I already feel tired from moving just a few times.

"How long?" I ask, keeping my words to a minimum, trying not to move my tongue. I think Amelia understands me, even if I do sound stupid.

"You've been asleep for three days. They've allowed me to look after you. Well, Nicholas said I could. The Duke, he said to leave you in your own filth. I don't like that man." She slaps her hand over her mouth. "Sorry," she whispers.

"I agree with you. Don't be sorry."

"I shouldn't say it, though." She looks up and around the room.

"Cameras," I say.

"Yes. The other brother told me to be careful."

"Other brother?" I'm confused.

She leans forward and whispers into my ear,

"William."

"You've seen him." I'm still trying not to move my tongue when I speak.

"He's been helping me look after you. He keeps to the side, so he can't be seen. He seems nice. A little inappropriate, the first thing he told me was that I had a bottom like a Kardashian. I'm assuming that's a nice compliment. He was smiling politely when he said it."

I try to stifle the laugh I feel, but when a little escapes, I regret it instantly. Damn, this pain's terrible.

"I don't think he's that good with social etiquette. He's nice, though." I give up on the no talking. The more I do it, the looser my mouth's feeling, and the taste of blood has gone. Of course, it could be that the painkillers have kicked in because my bottom suddenly seems to be less painful as well. "I can assure you that a Kardashian's bottom is a good one. Don't you know who they are?"

"Not really. I'm guessing they're celebrities, but I didn't really have a chance to follow all *that* growing up. My father made sure I was prepared for being Nicholas' wife."

"You knew this would happen?" I ask.

"Yes. Didn't you?" I shake my head. "It must've been

such a shock."

"Just a little. I've always been kept hidden away, but I didn't know why, until I came here. Makes perfect sense now."

She rolls her eyes.

"Yes, evidently, as women we're sexually wanton. Even allowing us to go to the library on our own will risk our virginity because of all the orgies we are likely to have on the way."

I laugh again — it hurts.

"Oh don't make me laugh."

"Sorry. The tasks are all prescribed in the documentation of this society — my father made me practice them, all my life. I went through every alternative." She goes quiet and looks at the striped rug on my bedroom floor.

"You've had this done to you." It hits me. "Every alternative. No punishment, locked in your room without food and water" –I gulp– "hit twenty times with a birch and the bridle?"

"He didn't use a birch. We didn't have one. He had a cane, though. It's only one stick instead of a few." She holds my hand.

"Still doesn't stop it from hurting any less or make it any more right. It angers me that these men think they can get away with doing this." I want to jump up from the bed and rant and rage. I want to storm to the nearest man with a horse whip, whack him across the back hundreds of times, and see how he likes it.

"Stay calm," Amelia pleads.

"We'll get through this. They won't always win." I move my hand so that it wraps around hers.

"I appreciate the sentiment, but I know what comes next. You don't."

Shit, I hadn't thought of that.

"Amelia?"

"We're lucky because we only have to do one task, but the original wife had to do all three. Fire, sex, death."

"Fire, sex, death," I repeat.

She looks up to where the camera is and shuts her eyes. I shuffle forward, ignoring the pain. If I can get some insight into what happens next, then I might be able to plan for it.

"You'll be fine. He won't give the one to you that'll destroy you. He loves you too much."

"What?" I'm baffled by her comment. "Amelia, what do you mean?"

She doesn't have a chance to answer me as the secret door in my room opens, and William appears from the shadows. His face is flushed red, and he is carrying a torch.

"You have to come now." He makes a grab for Amelia's hand.

"William?" She shakes him off.

"There's no time for arguments," he commands. "He knows she's awake."

Both of them look at me.

"What? Who knows I'm awake?"

"Good luck." Amelia allows William to lead her into the secret corridor.

"Good luck? With what? With whom?" I shout at them and wish I wasn't trapped in this bed, but my battered body won't allow me to move.

My bedroom door bursts open, and there's Nicholas. His brows are furrowed, and he looks like he's about to explode with anger.

"Cowards," I whisper to myself about William and Amelia and say a little pray to the pain gods to let me pass out again. I curse them in the next breath when I'm still awake. Oh well.

"Earl Lullington. What can I do for you?

CHAPTER EIGHTEEN

NICHOLAS

"You're awake." I storm into her room without waiting for admittance. She's sitting up in the bed, wearing pajamas over her bandages. Last time I saw her, she was naked and bleeding all over her sheets. Despite looking withdrawn from no food for a few days, she seems fine.

"I am. I woke not more than half an hour ago." She shuffles on the bed to get comfortable, and I can see that she's still in pain.

"Did Amelia give you the pills?" I ask.

"She did. I think they're starting to work as my body is more rested than when I first woke."

"You're to take them every four hours. I'll set a reminder on my phone to come and check that you've taken them." I pull my phone out of my pocket and pull up an alarm.

"There's no need. I'm sure I can manage to remember." She looks around the room for a clock — her face falling when she remembers that she doesn't have one. "Maybe I'll need that reminder."

My father decided when we were preparing the rooms for the girls that they wouldn't need clocks. He stated it would be better if they had no idea what time of day it was, other than by the rising and setting of the sun. It all sounded a bit more like adding additional torture into their stay to me.

"I'll have a clock put in here so you can keep an eye on the time yourself."

"Thank you, My Lord."

I grind my teeth at the form of address she uses for me.

"So, how are you feeling?" I'm still standing in the doorway. I can't bring myself to walk any farther into the room, yet. I want to strangle her for not saying 'yes' and thus preventing her body from being put through this. But at the same time, I want to kiss every inch of her body in the hope that it will stop the pain she's in. Argh. Women! Why do they have to be so complicated? Men are simple creatures, far more pliable. Particularly if you have a voracious dick like mine. Food, sleep, shower, shit, sex, not necessarily in that order, and several of those more than once a day.

"Just fine and dandy," she responds, and her own face darkens with anger.

"Why didn't you just say yes?" I can no longer temper my fury.

"Why should I? I'm not a liar, Nicholas."

"Because, if you did, then this would have been much easier, and I wouldn't have had to see you covered in blood and humiliated." I put my head in my hands and pull the strands of my hair through to the end. "I wouldn't have to worry that, because of what happened, you're broken."

She laughs at me. I see it hurts her, when she flinches, but she continues.

"You think this would break me? No, no chance. It's made me even more determined to make you see that what's happening here is wrong. You marry for love and with freedom of choice, Nicholas. If your wife misbehaves, you don't lead her around in some elaborate parade designed to humiliate her."

"You hate me." Her words hit me hard, and I want to go to her and hold her. I want to stroke her and make all the pain go away.

"No. I don't blame you for this. As I've said before,

you're weak. What happened to me is because of the society, and your father's macabre nature. What happens now is down to you, though."

I finally dare to move closer to her and sit on the edge of the bed. While she's speaking, she reaches out and takes my hand. I look at the cannula embedded in her delicate flesh.

"What do you mean?"

"Stop this. Go to your father and tell him you won't go through with it anymore. Tell him that you're letting Amelia, Elizabeth, and I go, and when you marry, it'll be for love. You're the only one who can do that. Does the title of Duke mean that much to you? Would you rather money and prestige over your soul?"

"I lost my soul years ago. There's still much that you don't know about this society and what it does."

"Then, tell me," she interrupts me.

"I'm too entwined in this. Bringing it down will destroy everything. William also. I can't risk his future."

"But you can mine?"

"It's not like that."

"Then what's it like?" She lets go of my hand and moves away to the other side of the bed.

"Victoria, please. Let's just finish the trials, let me get the title, and then, I can change things from there." I'm begging her. I lean forward and press a kiss to her lips. She doesn't respond, but she doesn't push me away, either. She sits there without moving.

"Are you in pain?" I go for her hand again, but she pulls it away. "Victoria."

"I want you to leave." She turns her head away, looking out of the barred window.

"Don't be like this. I'm not saying that I won't change things when I'm Duke. I'm just saying, for now, it has to be like this."

She doesn't reply.

"Talk to me," I demand.

"Leave." Her eyes are dead. I've seen affection for me in them before, despite the monster I am, but there's nothing there now. "You think after this there can ever be anything between us. If you put a stop to this now, then maybe, I could work on forgiving you, but you've seen me humiliated, beaten, almost killed, and still, you won't fight for me. You could've had my love Nicholas, but you've lost that. Just leave."

"Are you serious?" I jump off the bed, and she whimpers when the ripples from the force shake the mattress. "I don't have a choice. I have to do it this way. It's the only way to make sure everyone gets the future that will be best for them."

"You're deluded. If I carry on like this, then I'll have no future. I'll be dead."

"Then, just do the tasks — I'll give you the easy ones." Why does she have to be so complicated? I'm frustrated and fuming at the same time.

"And let Amelia and Elizabeth get beaten or worse instead."

"Don't ask this of me. Just accept what I say."

"I shouldn't need to ask you." She turns away. It's the final nail in our conversation. She won't acknowledge me anymore. I see that when she shuts her eyes.

"Fine, have it your way. Just don't come running back to me when this is over, and the society's gone." I go back to the door and slam it shut behind me, leaving her alone to wallow in her self-pity. Doesn't she realize this is hard for both of us? Damn frustrating, annoying women. Doesn't she understand how much it broke me to see her savagely beaten? I wanted to stop it the entire time, and it could've been prevented if she'd just said 'yes'.

I go straight back to my room. I'm shaking and sweating — I'm irate, and I'm worried. I don't know what to do with myself. I want to shut this thing down, now, but the pressure on me is incredible. I can't let my brother down. I can't let other girls go through what's happening to Victoria. I want it finished and done with. I want to go out and fuck an entire catalogue of lingerie models. Who the fuck am I kidding, no I don't? Sex is actually the furthest thing from my mind. In fact, I don't actually know what's going on in my mind. It's a muddle of confusion and suffering. I'm the devil — I must be. I have to be as bad as my father in order to beat him. I've done wrong things in my life. I've killed, maimed, and stolen, all in the name of this fucking society. This fucking society. I pick up a wooden framed chair next to me and throw it hard into a wall. It hits a mirror, which smashes into a thousand pieces on the floor. Next up, I swipe everything off my chest of drawers onto the floor. I stop short of the brandy, sitting temptingly in the decanter at the end. Reggie must've known that it would be something that I need. I pick it up, pull the stop out, and take in long gulps, which burn my throat. I drink half of the bottle. My head swims with the instant hit of the alcohol. Fuck. Argh. I pick up some priceless ornaments and throw them at the artwork adorning the walls. They may be worth millions, but I don't care. I want to get paralytically drunk and destroy. It's all I'm fit to do. It's all I'll ever do in this life. My father has told me enough times that I'll never beat him, and I'm starting to believe it. It is now that I need to go to the dark side of my brain, if that is even possible. Fuck everyone but William. I'll destroy this society. I down another load of the brandy, and its high alcohol content instantly mixes with my blood, which is already compromised from not eating since breakfast. I look at my clock. Dinner time. Maybe I can make myself pass out before anyone comes looking for me. I'm pretty confident that I'm halfway there.

The door to my room creaks. I spin around, and Elizabeth Sandford is standing there. She bites her lip and allows the sleeve of the dressing gown that she's wearing to fall from her shoulder.

"I heard a noise. I think my room must be underneath yours. I know we're not allowed up here, but I was worried."

She sashays up to me and places her hand on my chest.

"What's wrong, My Lord? Is it something I can help you with? You seem upset."

I look straight at her. She's swaying a bit, or is it the fact that I've downed pretty much a whole decanter of brandy in ten minutes?

"This must be hard for you as well. To see us women hurt in a manner than your sensitive nature dislikes. I've seen the true man you are underneath. You want to do this about as much as we want to be married off in this way. You want to love and have affection. Something your father took away from you with your mother. He killed her."

I grab her hand and pull it off my chest. I push her back but don't let go. "Don't talk about my mother. You know nothing about her."

"I know she left you all alone with the man who tortures you night and day. He wants to mold you into his likeness, but you have a heart. He'll never win." I don't know if she's deliberate or not in her words, but her voice is seductive. The gown slips a little farther revealing the gossamer silk of a bra covering the curve of her breast. My eyes flit to it and back to her face.

"You want to sleep with me?" I ask.

She purses her lips together.

"Who wouldn't? You're a handsome man."

"I won't have sex with you, no matter how much you try to flatter me with your false praise of my character, contrasting it with my father's. He's the devil, but he taught me everything he knows."

I let her hand go and bring my other hand to my mouth. It still contains the brandy bottle. I need more to numb everything. Tomorrow, I'll gather my strength and try to fight again. But tonight, I've nothing left. Two weeks ago, I was carefree, and I didn't have to think about this stupid society. Now, it's all my brain can focus on.

"There's another way." Elizabeth's voice permeates my thoughts.

She drops to her knees. "You want to lose your mind for a while. I can help you with that." Her hand is placed on my dick through my trousers, and before I have a chance to say no, she's undoing my zipper and removing me. I'm not hard. I don't know if it's the alcohol, or my lack of lust for the woman on her knees in front of me. But the second she brings my cock into her mouth, I lengthen and lose myself in the moment. Victoria was right — I have no soul.

CHAPTER NINETEEN

VICTORIA

Two weeks have passed since the day I was savagely beaten. I move a little better, but I know that I'll always bear the scars of my attack. Not just physically in the silver streaks that mar my perfect skin but also in the nightmares that haunt me. The names — I want to forget them, but no matter how much I try to fill my head with positive synonyms for women, the negative always seems to invade my consciousness. I see, now, despite the advent of feminism and the burning of bras, women are still second-class citizens within the nobility of England. I wonder how many others have been sold into a world of slavery as I have been.

"Victoria?" Amelia's voice drags me from my reflection. "Do you want anything else to eat?"

"Err. No, thank you. I'm good." I push half an American pancake to the side of my plate. I enjoyed the fruit, but I am still finding it hard to eat a lot. I've always prided myself on being toned and curvy, but with not eating and no swimming, I'm a shadow of my former self.

"Maybe we should ask Nicholas' doctor to retake a look at your tongue. He said you should be eating well by now. You didn't eat much dinner last night and not much breakfast."

"I'm fine. Honestly. Just not hungry. I ate all my fruit. I'm being healthy." I laugh, but she still frowns at me.

"Dear God, stop fussing over her all the time. If she'd

said yes, then she wouldn't be in the state she is." Elizabeth pipes into our conversation while shoving the last piece of her venison sausage into her mouth.

I haven't warmed to Elizabeth as I have Amelia. In fact, you could say I think she's a total bitch. She wants to marry Nicholas for the title and the money. That's completely obvious. I also question her morals — she doesn't seem to ask about anything that's going on here. Amelia doesn't make a show of hating her fate, but at least you can see she thinks it's wrong. With Elizabeth Sandford, you get the feeling she's enjoying what's happening. I shudder at that thought. Nobody could enjoy this.

"No one deserves what happened to Victoria," Amelia responds and wipes her mouth with a napkin.

"It's the rules — if she breaks them or doesn't answer in the way the Duke, or the Earl, demands of a wife, then she should be punished." Elizabeth picks up her coffee and takes a mouthful to wash down her breakfast.

"Were you aware of the tasks before coming here?" I ignore her misguided views and question her instead.

"Of course." She pouts.

"And you don't think that it's wrong?" I ask.

"Why should I? I'm a realist, not a dreamer like you."

"What's that supposed to mean?" Her words make no sense.

"We live in a male orientated world. If we want to succeed in it, we need to learn to be subservient."

"Why?" Amelia interjects.

"Because if we don't, then we'll end up with nothing."

"You do know that a woman can have a career of her own that doesn't involve opening her legs for a living, don't you?" I've had enough of this bitch.

"But it's a lot easier if you use what God gave you," she smirks. "Men are weak. They have one brain, and it isn't in their heads." She wiggles her index finger to illustrate a dick.

"Seriously, aren't you supposed to be a virgin?" Amelia snorts.

"You can still be a virgin and know how to give a man pleasure." She leans forward on her elbows. "Nicholas found that out two weeks ago."

I have my coffee cup halfway to my mouth while she's talking, but it never makes it there — I put it down with a thump.

"And what's that supposed to mean?"

"I sucked him off." She looks smug with her declaration I want to smack it off her face. I keep my calm, though. Mainly because moving fast still hurts. "He needed a release after all the stress that you're putting him through with your ridiculous acting out. I gave it to him. He's big — I gagged on him more than once. His cum is the sweetest I've ever tasted as well."

"Shut up," Amelia shouts at Elizabeth. I sit there dumbfounded. I know she isn't lying. I can see it in her eyes.

"I told him that he's welcome to come to me anytime he wants. It's one dick I won't ever say no to." Elizabeth carries on, and Amelia covers her ears, so she doesn't have to hear the conversation anymore. "If you don't want to end up dead, maybe, you should start showing him a few more favors of that kind," she sneers at me.

"I can't listen to this anymore. You're sick." Amelia stomps out of the kitchen. I push my chair back to go after her. I like the blonde, and I know talk of this will impact on her fragile emotions.

"You thought you had him wrapped round your little finger, didn't you?" Elizabeth stops my progress, and I swing back around to face her. "He called my name as he came. I've sucked enough men to know that, when they come, the name of the one they truly want is on their lips."

"I feel sorry for you." I step into her space. She instantly gets to her feet ready to fight me if needed. "You're the daughter of a Bishop and should have better morals. They seem to have disappeared down the drain with any compassion and kindness you might have. If you think that what's happening here is right and good for women, then you're as insane as the Duke and Earl. This is pure and simple kidnapping, murder, and then rape when he chooses a partner. When, not if, I get out of here, I'll see them all go to hell for this. Mark my words. If you want to get on your knees and suck Nicholas', no doubt, disease ridden dick, then go ahead. Open your legs and let him fuck you. I don't care. I hate him. If he chooses you as his wife, then I wish you the best of luck. In fact, congratulations, have him. I'd rather die than have him ever touch me again." Elizabeth's eyes go past me toward the doorway. I spin around and come face to face with Nicholas — his jaw ticking with anger.

CHAPTER TWENTY

NICHOLAS

"Elizabeth, leave," I order the smug woman out of my sight. Two weeks, two fucking weeks, I haven't seen Victoria. I thought that she might've grown a brain during that time, but it appears not.

"My apologies, My Lord, for you having to witness that appalling attack on your character." The jet-haired woman, who pleasured me the night of my drunken rampage, sways her hips seductively as she leaves the room where the girls were eating their breakfast. She runs a hand across my chest. I don't move. I allow the show of dominance from her because I see the look of jealousy that flits over Victoria's face. She quickly suppressed it, but I saw it. Too late — I have her. "If you need me, I'll be in my room. Try not to get beaten again, Victoria, I'd hate to delay the trials any further. I want to get on with my life and obtain my rightful position." Elizabeth sashays off down the corridor.

"Trailer trash bitch." Victoria coughs under her breath. I can't help the smirk that touches my lips because she's right. Elizabeth Sandford is a slut. She would make a terrible wife — she would fuck my entire retinue. I could never be sure that any children we had were mine. It isn't her fault, though. With a Bishop for a father, she was sexually repressed for years and has finally discovered her calling.

"Come here," I order Victoria — now that we're alone.

"Hell no." She takes a step farther away.

"Come here," I order again. This time with a little bit more force.

"Are you trying it on with all of us? I bet I was a big disappointment, seeing that you had to give to me rather than receive."

My lip lifts into a smirk again.

"You really are a freak. My god, you're actually enjoying this." She steps forward, this time, at a rapid pace and makes to go around me. I stand fully in the doorway, filling it with my muscular frame.

"You aren't going anywhere."

"I'm getting the hell away from you, and when I get out of here, I'm getting tested for STDs. You're probably a walking infection. Now, let me pass."

"You'd rather die than have me touch you again?"

"Yes." She makes a charge for me to try and get me to move out of the way. As she bounces off my taut body, I can see that she hurts herself more than she hurts me. "Get out of my fucking way."

"I didn't call her name, when I came."

She throws her hands up in the air.

"I don't want to hear this. Who you stick your dick into isn't my concern. As long as you keep that thing away from me, I'm happy."

"I mouthed yours because I was drunk — completely pissed off that you still weren't listening to me, and what I want you to do so that we can get through this together."

"Great, you were pissed at me, so you stuck your dick down another woman's throat. That really makes you a good candidate to be a husband. You say that you want to marry me, but what happens the first time we have an argument? You find the nearest willing hole and stick yourself in it." She tries again to get past me. "Will you get out of my fucking way?" She balls her fist and punches me in the jaw. It hurts — it actually causes me pain. Damn, she's strong for such a little thing.

"Argh," she cries. "God damn it." She grips her shoulder where, I know, the deepest of her wounds is. It must still be healing and was jolted when she hit me. "Please, just move."

"You know, for hitting me, I'm within my rights to put you back in the bridle."

Her eyes fill with worry, but her cheeks turn pink with fury.

"You have no rights over me. I'm a woman with my own thoughts and mind."

"You're my property — your father gave you to me," I snarl back.

"I'm a human being. I'm no one's property."

"Wrong. Until this is over, you're mine."

"Jerk." She tries one final time to get past me. I move out of the way at the last minute, and she goes flying by. I grab her arm and start to drag her down the hallway.

"Get off me."

"No."

"Nicholas, you're hurting me."

"I don't care. For once, you're going to listen to me."

"What's the point? You have nothing to say that would remotely interest me."

I pull her up the stairs toward my room. She digs her heels in.

"I can't go up there."

"My father's out. What I want to show you is up there."

"Thank God, you didn't say it was in your pants."

"You back on my dick again? I can show you that as well, if you want," I chuckle.

"Drop dead," she snarls.

I tug hard, and she has no choice but to follow me. Reggie appears from one of the rooms.

"Help me," Victoria screams.

I glare at him. He holds his hands up and steps back into the room.

"Jesus, all the men in this place are insane," Victoria huffs.

We get to my room, and I pull her inside, shutting the door and locking it, to give us privacy, I put the key into my pocket.

"I'm not going to sleep with you or suck you if that's why you've brought me up here. I mean it. You're holding me hostage and should be in prison."

"I know."

"What?"

"I should be in prison. I know you aren't going to sleep with me, but that doesn't stop me from wanting to touch you whenever you're in the same room as me. It doesn't stop me from wanting to seek you out to talk to you. In fact, you being my possession makes it even harder because I know that I can't have you." Both of us are breathing rapidly. Our gasps for air fill the sudden silence in the room

"Don't, please." Victoria's sweet tones finally break the tranquility.

"You're at an unfair disadvantage to the others. They seem to all know what happens next. You don't. They've already learned, from their fathers, what is required to become my wife. I want you to learn what's involved from a Duchess."

"Nicholas, there's no Duchess? Your mother, she's dead because of this." The word dead is stressed with such poignant emotion that I have a momentary regret that I'm about to share a part of my life with someone. I've hidden it away for so long, but this is Victoria. I've known since the moment I first saw her, staring intently at Van Gogh's Poppies, that there was something different about her. I've known that she'd be the one to break this curse, hanging over our families. I step up to a chest of drawers in my room and remove my mother's diary from it. I brought it up here a few days ago and have read the whole thing since.

"Here."

"What's this?"

She looks down at the silk cover as I push the book into her shaking hands.

"Open it and read a page."

"I don't think I should."

I roll my eyes.

"For once, in the short time we've known each other, accept that I'm trying to do something to help you. Please read the damn diary," I snap and plonk my weight down into a Queen Anne armchair. It's my favorite and, thankfully, survived the attack I made on my room. I place my head in my hands. I can feel a migraine simmering at the edges of my temples. This isn't how I thought my day would go. I hear the pages turn and look up. Victoria's flicking through the diary.

"Is this...?" she hesitates, so I answer for her.

"My mother's."

"Nicholas, I can't read this. It's personal to you and William."

"If it helps you in any way with what's to come next, then it's more pertinent to you. William and I have read it. We've mourned our mother, and what she was forced to do."

Victoria flicks through another few pages then gasps. I don't know what has elicited such a reaction because the whole diary's full of such moments.

She opens her mouth to speak and shuts it again.

"Read it."

"Fire, sex, death. That's what they called today. A death that's what I had. I'll never forget it, the pale face, the blood, the pain. Freedom, he was lucky. I wished for it. I

pray for it nightly, but it never comes. I'm in hell and became one of them today. There's no hope for me. I know he'll choose me. I see it in the way he looks at me. I'll have the last laugh, though. I'll end this — I'll conceive his son against my consent. The compassion that dies within me will be born into him. He'll rule and rid the world of the society of Oakfield."

When she finishes reading, Victoria closes the book and sits in her own chair.

"I don't know if I can read anymore."

"Take it with you. You need to prepare for tomorrow."

"Death? Nicholas, please tell me it isn't what I think it is?" she asks.

"I'm afraid toward the end my mother's words get a little jumbled. She wasn't in her right frame of mind."

"You've read this but still want me to go through with the trials?" I try to sense whether she's angry at that fact or sad, but I can't get a read on her.

"You should go." I pull the key out of my pocket and throw it toward her.

"Talk to me." She slides off the chair and picks the key up like it's a security blanket, but she's still hesitant and doesn't make a run for the door.

"I have to go through with this, Victoria. It's the only way. I can't let my mother die in vain. I can't risk William. I know I sound like I'm completely selfish, but please, read that and understand my point of view."

She looks down at the diary again.

"Thank you."

I shut my eyes and listen to her put the key into the lock, turn it, and leave the room. I'm no good at verbalizing what I'm feeling, but hopefully my mother can, in some way, show Victoria why I need to finish this properly. I need to take the title from my father and make everything right for William, for my mother, and for all the other girls who've been harmed over two hundred years of the Oakfield society. Even if it's to the detriment of the woman I'm falling in love with.

"You know — I can look after myself — I'm not that incapable. I could walk out of this place tomorrow if I wanted to." The hidden doorway behind me creaks, and William's voice comes through it.

"Your sense of direction's awful. You'll get lost before you get to the end of the driveway," I retort with a weary laugh.

"I'm not that bad. Better than you are. You got lost going out for Chinese once."

"They'd changed premises."

"No excuse."

He slaps me on the shoulder, and I sit up.

"What are you doing here?"

"Keeping hidden but seeing things again. You gave her mum's diary?" He pulls up a chair and sits next to me.

"I thought it might help her understand why I need to do things this way."

He snorts, and his tics appear. He strokes the side of his face, nose, and taps twice on the arm of the chair.

"William?"

"Listen. I meant what I said. If I chose to walk out of here, I would be alright. You should fight for Victoria over me. I know she frustrates the hell out of you, but I'm not a fool. I see the growing feelings between you both, despite the situation."

"Stop it," I command and take his hand to stop him from tapping on the chair. He taps on my fingers instead. "This is stressing you. I made a promise to you and Mum. I'll always be there to help you and protect you from our father."

"You were five years old. I don't even remember the

promise. I was three."

"But I still made it," I interrupt.

"What if you don't succeed?"

"Then, I'll die for the cause. I won't allow another woman to go through this. Any children I may be lucky enough to have will choose their wives the conventional way. They'll go on dates and have their hearts' broken."

"Not heartbreak. Isn't that what women have and demand ice cream for all the time?"

"It is, but I'd never say that to them."

"Maybe I should ask Victoria if she want's ice cream while she's reading the diary?"

"William?" Because of his autism, my brother isn't always aware of the social norms. "That's not a good idea. You should probably stay away from her for a while. I'm not sure how she'll react to the diary."

"Joke, brother. I miss you smiling at me. I know that she needs time alone. I don't always understand everything, and I think that gazing at the stars is a lot easier than interacting with society. But, somehow, I have this built-in instinct when it comes to understanding women."

"You need to share that with me, then."

"You're doing well. The diary was the right decision."

There's a knock on my door. William freezes.

"Who is it?"

"Mr. Hane, My Lord."

My butler, thank god. "Come in."

He enters and bows to us.

"Hello, Lord William."

"Reggie." My brother gets to his feet and, without an understanding of personal space, embraces my butler with warm affection.

"William put the man down." I also get to my feet and pull my brother off.

"Sorry to disturb you. I've just had word from His

Grace. He's to return home within the hour. He's sent the call out to the society members. No more waiting. You're all to be in the banqueting room for his return. The next trials will be happening then and there."

CHAPTER TWENTY-ONE

VICTORIA

I can barely read the pages before me for the tears that stream down my face. This is a diary written by someone who'd been through what I'm going through, and that someone was Nicholas' Mother. My heart breaks, but I'm still confused. If he's read this, then why didn't he put a stop to it? Is he that conflicted and controlled by his father that he can't see what's right and wrong. I want to go back to him and tell him that it'll all be okay if he stops this now. The world won't fall apart — he and William will be safe, but something sits uneasily in my stomach. I don't know everything that's going on here. I must read more. Firstly, though, I need to make a preference for the next trial, 'fire, sex, death'. I read a small passage about it earlier but didn't finish it when I came to my room. I wanted to start the diary from the beginning, so I got the whole picture. I flip to where I know it begins.

'Fire, sex, and death is the hardest task of them all. It's designed to break the weakest of the women who haven't already been destroyed by the punishment task. I was whipped, as you know dear diary, but nothing can prepare you for what you become when these tasks are handed out.'

My bedroom door flies open before I can read any further. I shove the diary under my pillow and glare at the Duke's guards.

"I thought our rooms were sacred."

“Maybe the others are, but yours is a whole different state of affairs. Get up, now.”

“Go to hell.” I ignore the twerp in the Duke’s livery. They don’t command me.

“Get up, or I'll drag you by the hair to complete the next task.” He menacingly steps forward.

“The next task?” Shit, I think. I haven’t had a chance to read all about it yet.

“Yes, it’s time. Get up.”

My legs suddenly feel as though they’re ten ton weights. The words, ‘fire, sex, death' are resonating through my head in a loop that sounds more imposing with every repeat. I manage to stand. I’m not sure how.

“I’m up.”

“Follow me, then,” the guard sneers and leads off. I want to run away into the hidden passages in the house and hope I can find a way out, but I know it will be futile. I’ll be dragged out and probably put in the bridle. I have solid plans to never go in there again, so I follow him. Halfway down the corridor, Amelia leaves her room. She looks like a ghost. She’s deathly pale and shaking like a leaf. Over the last few days, she’s had an air of calm about her, but not now.

“Amelia?” I grab her hand to check that she’s alright.

“No talking!” the guard shouts at me.

“Fuck you,” I respond, not caring about punishment.

“Are you alright?”

She opens her mouth to speak, but the guard grabs me by the hair, before she has a chance. He pulls me into the room where the Duke’s waiting and throws me to the floor in front of him.

“The bridle didn’t work. She’s disobeying the orders.”

“I’m checking my friend is alright,” I shout back at him and go to get up. I’m pushed back down.

"I like her at my feet. It's a good position for someone with a mouth like hers. Actually, no, on her knees sucking my dick would be better." The Duke laughs at his own comment. Nicholas comes into view, and he's not smiling. He looks tired and angry.

"The girls are mine. You can't touch them without my permission." He ignores me and vents his anger on his father instead.

"I shared your mother with my father and brother — why change tradition?" the Duke snarls back. I see Nicholas' fist form into a ball, ready to lash out, and my stomach turns with overwhelming nausea, at the statement.

"It's one tradition I can change without the society's consent, and I'm changing it now. None of these girls are to be touched without my permission. If I find out that they have, then you'll be tried by the society for corrupting the succession process. Something I know you take seriously because of the consequences." Nicholas is fuming, but it's the first time I've seen him stand up to his father, and the Duke actually backs down. The older Cavendish huffs and steps away to the side.

"Let the next trial begin." The Duke holds his hand up and thumps it down on a table.

"Ladies, my son has already determined the level of discipline that will be required to correct you, as his wife. Some needing more than others." He looks at me, and I can't help it — I sneer while getting to my feet. "As the Duchess of Oakfield, you'll have to set an example. You'll be called upon to accompany the Duke to social functions, which will contain a variety of people, including royalty. You'll be expected to act with the highest decorum at all times. That's not all that will be demanded of you, though. The society's a business — we undertake certain deals on behalf of the members to further our ambitions. You'll be required to take part in this as much as necessary. This is the purpose of these three trials." The Duke walks over to a sunken area in the hall. I'd noticed it before but never thought much of it. Four guards line up around the corners of the area, and the Duke nods. A cover's pulled back, and a pit of burning coal is revealed.

"To join the society, one of the tasks is to walk over hot coals. It's supposed to signify the age old tradition of being willing to do anything for advancement. One of you ladies will be given that task by Earl Lullington." The Duke looks at his son and motions for him to step forward and take the stage. I notice for the first time how tired Nicholas seems. He has dark circles under his eyes, and the stubble lining his chiseled jaw is longer than usual. A few more days of growth, and he'll have a somewhat unkempt beard. He still wears a suit, which is immaculately pressed, but somehow it doesn't hang on his shoulders with the arrogant confidence that it would have done a few weeks ago. I want to go to him, embrace him, tell him it'll be alright, and that the world isn't really falling apart. But I know that it is, and I've already promised him that I wouldn't lie. The sound of my name on Nicholas' deep tones draws me from my reflection.

"Victoria will walk the coals," he says.

"I'll do what?" I exclaim loudly in shock.

He glares at me. It's a look that tells me to keep my mouth shut. 'Fire, Sex, Death' pops into my head. Ok, maybe I'll be silent as this is apparently the fire, and I like the sound of the other two a lot less than walking over hot coals.

"How very disappointing," the Duke moans. "I was hoping that you would choose her for sex. I was looking forward to it." He laughs this time, and I look to Amelia. Seeing that she's close to tears, I reach out and take her hand. She grips mine back tightly, saying nothing as the

Duke starts up with his annoying sermons again.

"In all ways, the wife of a Duke must be completely faithful to her husband, unless, for reasons known only to the Duke, he commands her to personally commit carnal acts with another person. I did this with my wife. I wanted to work with a particular client, so I gave him a night with my wife to seal the deal." He chuckles, and my blood freezes. "She didn't come back *too* bruised." I look at Nicholas as he stumbles back, grabbing a nearby chair to support himself. I'm sure his father enjoys teasing him. I look up to the hidden alcoves and wonder if William is listening to this as well. It must be hard on them both to know that their mother was brutally treated and chose death over being with them in life. That she couldn't try to save them from the fate they faced. I will Nicholas to walk out and tell his father that he'll not do this, but I know it won't happen because this is the only way he can see to put an end to everything.

"For the purpose of this task, I get to have a little fun." The Duke stands proudly, and I have a horrible sinking feeling I know what's coming. "The chosen lady will be given to me by my son to complete fellatio. If you, in anyway, attempt to bite my penis, then I'll have your teeth pulled out of your mouth, one by one, without anesthetic. A good wife needs to obey her husband no matter what. Your body's his property, and he can command how you use it."

I can't help but be over the moon at not having to complete that task. I like my teeth in my mouth, and I would definitely lose them because I wouldn't be able to prevent myself from trying gnaw off the Duke's gross dick. It would be the safest way of ensuring I didn't get any nasty diseases.

"Nicholas, who do you choose for this task?" the Duke asks, and I send up a silent prayer that he doesn't choose Amelia. It's already been proven that Elizabeth's a whore, so give her that task. I'm sure she'll enjoy it. She can compare father and son. Yuck! What a disgusting thought.

"Elizabeth. I happen to know that she has talents that you'll rather appreciate."

The assembled crowd murmur amongst themselves, but my attention's distracted when Amelia grips my hand even tighter and whispers,

"Thank you for being my friend. You've a strength I've never seen before. I know that you'll be the last Duchess of Oakfield to be chosen this way."

"What?" I ask, but the Duke interrupts us again. This time, I'm pulled away to the coals by the guards. Amelia's taken up to the front of the stage, and Elizabeth's pushed to her knees at the Duke's feet.

"The final task, which Amelia will complete, is the ultimate sin for both husband and wife. The society is brutal — as many of you know from the punishments you've received for misdemeanors. If you betray us, then the punishment is death. Public execution. No second chances. As wife to my son, you'll be expected to uphold this. You'll be expected to kill."

The bottom falls out of my world when I see a gun is placed in front of Amelia. No. No. Her words suddenly start to make sense. The only task she couldn't complete. I'm being held by the two guards, but I get free from them with unimaginable strength and throw myself at Nicholas' feet. He looks down in shock, and with an almost silent voice, I whisper,

"Swap Amelia and I — I want to do the killing."

CHAPTER TWENTY-TWO

NICHOLAS

"What are you doing? Get up." I stare down dumbstruck at Victoria. "Have you gone insane? I gave you the easiest task." I bend down and, with gritted teeth, tell her to stop this madness.

"No. I want to kill the person." All the time she speaks, her eyes are flicking over to Amelia.

"I'm not going to give you the gun. Go back to the coals."

"What's going on?" My father shouts from the other side of the room. He's already undoing his trousers and pulling himself out. It's not something I enjoy seeing, but sadly it's something I've witnessed far too often. The society's members are infamous for their orgy nights. The one and only thing that I used to quite enjoy.

"Nothing," I reply.

"Can the bitch not even do the easiest of the tasks without causing a problem? George" –he waves his hand in the air toward one of the guards– "bring the scold's bridle. I don't have time for messing around." My father shoves his dick into Elizabeth's mouth, and she gags around the surprise intrusion. "I hope you're going to be better at swallowing me than that."

"It's fine. I'll deal with it. We don't need the bridle." I pull Victoria up toward me. "Stop this now. I thought giving you the diary would have knocked some sense into you."

"Please swap us," she pleads. I can see the desperation in her eyes.

"Tell me why? Give me one good reason. You know what's about to happen. I don't want that on your conscience."

"Amelia." She opens her mouth to tell me, but there's a commotion at the door. A man's brought in and thrown onto his knees in the center of the room. He's one of the 'workers', as we call them here in the society, who do the mundane work for us. They aren't paid well, for they're the lowest of the low. Pulled from the streets and offered a better life only to be thrown to the lion, that is my father, and forced to risk everything, so we don't have to.

"This man has stolen from us. He took money to perform a task, and he spent it on getting high instead. The work was not done to the highest standard, and I now have to get another loyal man out of prison in Egypt, as a result." My father's bucking his hips into Elizabeth's mouth while he speaks. He's using her like a rag doll with a hole to get himself off. There's no finesse about the act. It's raw fucking of a willing hole. Then again, that's pretty much all Elizabeth Sandford is: willing with three holes to stick a dick in. "The punishment for stealing from us is death. Sometimes, as the leader, we don't like to get our hands dirty, and that's where our wives come into the equation. Amelia, your task is to kill this man."

Victoria whimpers and grabs hold of my ankle. "Please, don't make her do this."

"You know I have to follow the rules," I respond.

"Let the games begin," my father shouts.

"Nicholas, please."

"Enough," I shout and grab Victoria by the arm. I drag her to her feet and, with the red mists descending, pull her across the room back to the coals. Behind me, I can hear one of the guards explaining to Amelia how to use the gun. To the side of me is my father's carnal grunts, and Elizabeth's wet suction. All the time, Victoria is squirming in my hands.

"No!" she screams, but I slam my hand over her mouth to muffle the sound.

"Damn it, please stop this. Just do what I ask. I can't handle this with every task. Why are you so bloody defiant all the time?"

"Kill him." My father's voice echoes around the room. "His punishment is death."

"Please don't," the man whimpers. The gun cocks.

Victoria's wriggling so much in my arms that I can barely hold her. She's like a piece of Jell-O. She bites on the hand I have clamped over her mouth, and I curse.

"Fuck."

I've had enough and push her onto the coals, so she has no choice but to walk on them. She's still defiant, though, as she stumbles back across them toward and then past me. I spin on my heels. The world turns slowly like those old-fashioned movies where the film breaks, and the world turns like it would go on forever. Victoria falls to her feet and screams. At the same time Amelia puts the gun in her mouth and pulls the trigger, ending her life as her head explodes.

"No!" Victoria cries out, again and again, bringing the world rapidly back up to speed. I can barely catch my breath as Amelia's body falls to the floor next to the drugged up thief that she was supposed to kill. Suddenly, I'm running. I'm next to Victoria, scooping her up into my arms. My father's sexual grunts come back into my consciousness as he comes down Elizabeth's throat. I feel sick — I'm going to be sick. The stench of death fills the room. Blood is flowing all over the floor — parts of the dead girl's brain and skull are splattered everywhere. And still, my father comes and comes. I can't do this. I need to leave. My legs are carrying me, and I hold a still hysterical Victoria in my arms. We're going —

we're getting out of here.

"Leaving so soon, son?" my father calls out. A gun goes off again. I turn back to see Elizabeth Sandford holding the smoking weapon, this time, and the condemned man lying dead beside Amelia.

"At least, the tasks were completed, and we're one girl down. Makes the choice a whole lot easier, don't you think?"

I don't wait to hear any more. I just get the hell out of there.

CHAPTER TWENTY-THREE

VICTORIA

Nicholas carries me out of the house and races toward a car. I'm still shaking. The only task that she could never complete. Her father had asked her to commit murder before, and she'd naturally refused. I dread to think the punishment she must've received from him. Whatever it was broke her enough that I just watched her commit suicide. I bury my head into Nicholas' chest as he shouts instructions to a liveried man.

"Give me the keys."

"My Lord, this is your father's car. If you wait a moment, I'll get one of yours."

"Just give me the fucking keys." Nicholas gently places me down against the midnight blue Land Rover. "Wait there," he orders. I don't think I could move if I tried. My legs are like jelly, and I use the car to hold me up. Nicholas spins around and stomps over to the guards. He pulls his hand back and floors the surprised man with one punch. He picks the keys out of the livery man's hand and clicks open the car. "Get in." I obey. He goes to the driver's side and gets in. He puts his seatbelt on, and I do the same before he takes off, speeding down the long driveway.

"Nicholas." I reach out and touch his leg, but he doesn't respond. He just focuses on the massive gateway in front of us. It starts to open — alerted, no doubt, by a sensor in the car. He's going to take me away from here. I squeeze his leg a little harder. His breathing's getting quicker and quicker. "Nicholas," I reassure again as the gate finishes opening. The path to freedom is laid bare before us, but at the last minute, he slams his foot down on the break. The car skids sideways over a manicured lawn and halts just before a garish statue of a little girl entwined with a snake. He bangs his hands on the steering wheel and gets out of the car and starts to beat the crap out of it. The thumping of the metal makes me shudder. He's falling apart before me. I undo my seat belt and slide across and out his side. He's going mad — the strength of his fury is so great that dents are appearing on the Land Rover. Without thinking, I step closer to him and wrap my hands around his waist. I'm standing behind him, and he stills. I can hear his heavy gasping breaths. I lay my head against his back and hear the anguished cries wracking his body.

"I killed her," he laments.

"No,"

"I didn't listen to you. I killed her. I want to take you away from here, but I can't. I should be able to drive through that gateway, but I can't. I'm going to kill you as well." He turns around, and I can see the tears falling down his face. I step up on the balls of my feet and use my thumb to wipe them away.

"You didn't kill her. The society did. She never had any hope. She told me that her father had been preparing her for the trials since she was young. He was abusing her and hiding behind what this society is. She was broken. You didn't kill her. The murder was the one task that she could never complete. She'd rather go to heaven with her conscience clear."

"I should have seen how broken she was. I knew she wasn't right, but I thought it was the stress of the situation."

I shake my head.

"She was a dead woman walking. I don't think anyone could have saved her, no matter how much we wanted to." I feel sick. Amelia was only twenty-one and had known nothing but abuse all her life. "Her father is a vile man, and I won't rest until he's punished for this."

"Neither of us will."

I look over to the gateway. I could push off Nicholas and make a break for my freedom, but I'm pulled closer to him by the situation we're in. Somewhere, in all of this, I've developed feelings for my captor.

"William," Nicholas speaks.

"I won't risk him. We're going to finish this together." I step back and slide my hand down to his, so he can lead me back to the car.

"Victoria." He doesn't move. "Marry me?"

"What?"

"Marry me?"

I can't find the answer I want to give — my throat goes dry. Most people would think that I'm insane for even considering this, but I am. I'm in love with him and all that he wants to do. He's been in the worst position just as I have. We've both been oppressed and forced against our wills to conduct acts that have left us confused and hurting, but together, we've discovered we can beat our devils. Together we'll win.

"Make me your woman first."

"What?"

I step up on the balls of my feet again and press a soft kiss to his lips.

"Stop the pain in my chest — stop my heart from breaking at all the death and hate around us. Show me what love is."

He crushes his lips to mine, apparently not needing to be asked twice, to show me what pleasure feels like. Before long, I'm lifted up into his arms, and we're moving. Our lips part.

"Where are we going?"

"There's a summer house a short walk away. I want

you privately, not in the middle of the driveway with the rest of the society leaving."

"Good idea." I join our lips again, and we stumble, well Nicholas stumbles, through the gardens to the summer house. The smell of roses hits me, and I pull back. Nicholas puts me down on my feet and opens the door. The summer house is filled with highly fragrant blooms. I pick a vibrant red rose and twirl it around in my fingers.

"They're my favorite flowers. The garden where I grew up had loads of them." Memories of my father being the one to put me in this position surface, and a tear escapes my eye.

"Wait here," Nicholas orders and disappears back outside. I take a look around. It's small and secluded — a place for bringing a book and lounging on the daybed in the center of the room. White blinds are at all the windows, but this place is private, and they don't need to be drawn. The daybed is covered in a white blanket. Oakfield Hall is masculine to the extreme, but this place is feminine. Nicholas returns with a few more roses in his hands. He pulls the petals off and strews them over the bed.

"This place isn't like the rest of Oakfield Hall."

"No, my mother had it built. She wanted a place to escape when my father had his mistresses over. He at least did one nice thing for her."

He pats the bed for me to go to him. I do and stand between his legs.

"Are you sure you want to do this?" he asks.

"Am I sure I want you to strip me naked and make love to me, or fuck me? However, it is you roll." I chuckle to diffuse the sudden tension that pools in my stomach.

"This is your first time. I'm going to be gentle. The fucking can come later."

"Sounds good to me."

He reaches up and strokes my face.

"Things will change."

"I know."

"She won't have died in vain."

"We'll always honor her."

I lean forward, and we kiss slowly. He pulls me onto the bed and lays me down.

We part lips, and he pulls the t-shirt that I'm wearing over my head. I sit up a little, so he can remove my bra. I'm not big breasted, but that doesn't seem to bother Nicholas as he instantly buries his head between them.

"Delicious." He flicks my nipple, and I moan low in my throat. I've always had a sensitive body, but around Nicholas, everything seems to double in sensation. I'm vibrating underneath him with the need for more. He flips me over and places the same kisses on my back. I feel him tense when he sees some of the bruising and deeper wounds, which haven't fully healed, yet. He pays particular attention to them as if apologizing for being a part of their infliction. I've long since forgiven him.

My jeans are next to be removed and then my knickers. He steps back and drops his suit jacket to the floor. I've never seen him without it and lick my lips at the sight. He pulls the left sleeve of his shirt toward him and unhooks the cufflink. He places it on a table, next to the daybed, and does the same with the other one.

"Do you always wear suits?" I ask while he removes his shirt and places that on the table as well. I take in his chest. It's defined with chiseled muscles and taper's down to a place of hidden promises in his trousers.

"I feel like I have, lately. I prefer jeans and a t-shirt, but unfortunately the position often requires a certain dress code."

"I want to see you in jeans," I blurt out, and he smiles. "Are you liking what you see, Victoria?"

"Maybe," I tease.

"Well, how about this?" He undoes his belt and then the zipper of his trousers, which he then lowers. Between my thighs starts to throb just at the sight of him in tight boxers. He kicks off his shoes and removes his trousers and socks. Next thing I know, he's back on top of me, kissing down my body.

"Isn't the underwear coming off?" I ask.

"Soon. If I take them off right now, I won't be able to take this slowly. I'm not going to risk hurting you *anymore*." The 'anymore' is said with poignant emotion. I need to reassure him that I'm not going to fall apart.

"I'm not broken. You've made me stronger, if anything."

"I'm still not prepared to risk that fact when it comes to carnal activities. Now shush and let me be the master here. I want to make you feel good."

I lay back and shut my eyes as Nicholas puts his head between my thighs. Before long, I'm coming on his face in a much-needed release. I know I'm mourning the loss of my friend, but she's been the catalyst to bring about change. No more women will be harmed as a result of the sacrifices that she's made in her life.

Nicholas slides up my body and kisses my lips. He tastes of me, and it's decadent and totally wicked. I forget, for a second, who I am and why I'm here.

"Last chance to say no." His eyes flicker with fear, a concern that he'll hurt me or worse.

"I'm beginning to think you don't want me as much as you say," I taunt.

He raises a playful eyebrow while grabbing the waistband of his boxers and pulling them down his legs. Holy fuck! My eyes almost bug out of my head at the sight of him naked. It's like one of the Greek gods in the paintings that adorn the walls of Oakfield Hall, except he's so much better endowed. His cock struts out from his torso, covered in clear liquid at the tip. He's ready for me already.

"I'm going to hurt you, at first. It's unavoidable. I was blessed with girth."

I chuckle at his formal use of words.

"It's a pretty big dick."

He shakes his head and positions himself at my entrance.

I lay back and allow my hands to entwine in the sheets when he pushes in. He wasn't joking when he said he had girth. I breathe through the discomfort until the pleasure takes over again, and I relax around his intrusion.

"Move, please," I pant, and he obeys. In a slow, tantalizing movement, he withdraws from me and pushes straight back in.

"Move." I shut my eyes and allow my head to fall back. I'm no longer a virgin. I've broken the rules: joined with the man I was given to, and I don't care. All I want is for him to move faster. To fuck me. I rotate my hips to encourage him, and he grunts out a strained response.

"Victoria, don't tempt me. I'm struggling to be gentle."

"Haven't you learned, yet. I don't break easily. Fuck me."

He moans deeper, and his pupils dilate to the pitch of the darkest night. The devil is released, and I'm pleased. He pulls his hips back and slams into me. The force sends me up the bed and an explosion rocks through my body. I'm coming again, already. Nicholas continues his thrusts as I reach my precipice and fall over. I'm flying in his arms as he fucks me like a wild animal. I'm raw and loving every moment. My lover buries himself, deeply, inside me and stills. He comes with a loud raspy call of my name. I feel the jets of seed flood my womb.

Fuck, he's bare. No condom. He must see the moment that I worry, for he bends and kisses my lips.

"I'm clean, and you're protected. You have my word on this."

I relax again. Nicholas withdraws from me, and we entwine our limbs on the daybed. He pulls a blanket over us.

"Are you alright?" he asks.

"I feel different," I respond.

"Is that a good or bad different?" He looks worried and sits up a bit.

"Good. I made a decision for myself. It's probably the first time ever."

His face softens, again, and he lays back down. "Do you want to make another one? I asked you a question before."

"You did."

"Will you help me end this for good? Will you be my wife?"

"Yes," I answer — confident that I'm doing the right thing.

CHAPTER TWENTY-FOUR

NICHOLAS

I watch Victoria sleeping — she looks peaceful. It's nice to watch her in person and not via a monitor. She opens her mouth and mumbles something about an oat and raisin cookie and then wiggles her perfect nose. I smile because I'm relaxed and happy. I've never enjoyed watching a woman this way before. It's been sex and goodbye, but with Victoria, it's different. After we made love twice more, we laid in each other's arms and talked about our childhood for a few hours. She fell asleep, but I wasn't tired. I've got far too much on my mind and none of it good. No matter what Victoria says, I'm responsible for Amelia's death. All this has been for my succession. I could have said no and walked away, but I didn't because of William and my fears for myself. I was selfish but no more. Together, Victoria and I will finish this. I slide from the bed and fumble around for my boxers. I eventually find them slung over a vase of fake roses. The flowers are everywhere. It's as if my mother knew that the girl I would fall for would pick them as her favorite. Tiptoeing quietly, I grab the rest of my clothes and go outside. I need some air to think about what happens next. I pull my phone out of my pocket and dial Reggie's number. He may be my butler, but he's also a confidant.

"My Lord, where are you?" he answers after the first ring.

"My mother's summer house."

I can hear him exhale a sigh of relief.

"You didn't leave. What about Victoria?"

"She's with me."

"You have spent time together?"

"If you're asking if we've slept together, then yes. I've made my decision — I'm going to marry her. It may not have a been a traditional courtship, but she's everything that I want in a wife. Together, we'll disband the society and see that no more girls are hurt by its rules."

He goes silent on the other end of the phone.

"Reggie."

"I'll help you in any way I can. It won't be easy. Your father is already putting things in place. He'll check Miss Victoria, the moment you return, to confirm that her virginity is still intact. You and I are both aware of the consequences when he finds out that it isn't."

"He won't touch her."

"You have to think carefully, My Lord."

"Is he at home?"

"No. He left after Miss Amelia's body was removed to her father." I wince at the mention of Victoria's dead friend.

"Did he take it?"

"No, she's caused shame on her family, and he refused her back. Your father has had her placed in the cellar until something can be done."

"I want you to make arrangements for her to be buried in the local church. They'll not ask any questions. They're used to random bodies suddenly appearing."

"I'll sort it at once, My Lord."

"Thank you, Reggie. Where's my father?"

"He went to his flat." I don't need to ask what my butler means by his flat. It's the place where he goes when he wants time to fuck in peace, away from Oakfield, even if it's still on the grounds.

"I need to go check on Victoria. I don't want to leave her for long. Can you send some food and clean clothing down here for her? I'm going to go and see my father. I want a guard as well, make that two. One for William and one for her. I know you have contacts."

"I do, Sir. I'll sort it at once."

"Thank you."

I hang up, and the summer house door opens. Victoria stands there, rubbing her eyes. She has the sheet wrapped around her body.

"I wondered where you'd gone?"

"I was just talking to my butler. My father has left Oakfield, but that doesn't mean you're safe. I don't know his next move, but I do know that the second he gets hold of you he'll have you before his doctor, again. That's not happening. I need to go and speak to him. Tell him I've made my decision. I want you to stay here. My butler has contacts. He's going to get someone to guard you and someone for William, also."

"Nicholas." She places her hand on my chest. "I've been thinking. We should run away — go to Scotland and marry. He can't do anything about it once we're man and wife. You'll be married, and he'll need to step aside. Then, we can start changing the rules."

"I wish it were that easy." I pull her closely to me and press a kiss to her sex tangled hair.

"Your father and the rules."

"The last task."

"What is it?"

"The one that's essential to the society's business. It's the one that defines us."

"I don't understand?"

I take a deep breath and lead Victoria back into the summer house. We take a seat on the daybed.

"You know you asked me about the Van Gogh picture in the main hall." I run a hand through my hair with the nerves I feel.

"Yes. The obvious fake."

"It's not a fake. It's the real one."

"But that can't be possible. It was stolen eight years ago." She screws her nose up in confusion.

"I know. I was the one who stole it."

"What?" She pulls back from me like I've just told her that her favorite puppy has died, or something. She's in shock and confused. "You stole it? The real 'Poppies', you have the real painting in your hall."

"Yes." I nod guiltily.

"How?" she exclaims.

"I've been trained as a thief since almost the day I was born. Most of the members of the society are. Nobody suspects us because of who we are. We have a lot more pictures in our collection than are on show. Most of the stolen Nazi pictures are hidden in special storage under Oakfield Hall. We're worth billions in collectable art."

Victoria slides from the bed and puts distance between us.

"And that's why the society was set up. To collect art. We needed money to maintain our positions. It was the one-way way to do it that the founders all agreed on. Over the years, to keep us going, we've allowed others who possess the appropriate skills to join. The majority of work is still the acquisition of paintings, but we also collect sculptures, architecture when we can steal it, and famous photographs and videos."

"I can't believe what I'm hearing."

"Are you angry?"

"I'm confused. You steal paintings and think it gives you the right to treat women the way you do?" She looks at me, eyes narrowed, and the expression on her face is harsh.

"When the society was set up, my ancestors were the highest ranked. They took on the most risk. In those days, losing their head would've been the least of their problems if they were caught. My four times great grandfather demanded something in exchange. He wanted a choice of brides for his son. The rules and trials were documented and have been in place ever since. My great, great grandfather tried to repeal them during the Victorian times, but the industry was exploding, and the artworks collected were being used for expanding the society's interests during the Industrial Revolution. New rules were put in place stating that should we try to stop the legacy of our succession, we'd forfeit everything, including our lives. The Dukedom of Oakfield would become extinct because all heirs would be executed. That's why I've fought so hard against this. Not only would I die but also William. He's an innocent in this. His only crime is having the father that he does."

Victoria squeezes me a little harder when I finish my mini-speech.

"The decisions of our ancestors have put us in the position we're in. We'll work together to try and put a stop to it. I'll trust your decisions. But, when we succeed, we must give the artwork back. It's not ours to keep." She sits down on the bed again. Her legs seeming too heavy to support her weary frame.

"Even 'The Poppies'? I'm quite fond of that one. I nearly got caught taking it."

She frowns.

"*Even* 'The Poppies'. When this is over, you can tell me about how you took it. I'm actually intrigued.

I bend down, kiss her and let go to search out the rest of my clothes.

I have to go and find my father. I need to tell him we're marrying."

"Is he going to make me do the last task?" she questions.

"I don't know, but if he does, I'll do all I can to help you. Trust your instincts."

"What is it?"

I nervously lick my lips.

"You'll have to steal a painting."

CHAPTER TWENTY-FIVE

NICHOLAS

It doesn't take me long to get to my father's other residence. It's on the other side of the estate. It's the place he takes the whores, and judging by the noise coming from his bedroom, he's already at it with one. I swallow down the bile that comes from hearing the screams.

"Tell him I want to speak to him, now," I growl toward a guard who's conflicted about what he should do. It's a case of deciding which devil is worse between my father and me, at the moment. The fact that my fist is inches from breaking his nose forces his hand, and he scuttles up the stairs to interrupt my father's pleasures. I settle myself into a chair and wait impatiently

"Nicholas." My father saunters down the stairs in what I suspect is nothing more than a housecoat. "I was in the middle of something rather important. What's it you want? And what have you done with the girl?"

He walks straight past me and pours himself a glass of red wine from a decanter on the table.

"She's somewhere safe."

"You'll have her back at Oakfield Hall by dusk, and I'll have Doctor Fallen confirm that you've treated her honorably. I know your reputation."

"It's no different to yours," I snap back and jump to my feet.

"I think my satisfaction rates are much higher than yours."

"No, your hospitalization rates are more widely known than mine. There's a difference. Does the whore upstairs know what she's letting herself in for?"

He smirks.

"Oh, she's fully aware and looking forward to it."

"She's insane."

He laughs.

"Just say what you've come here to say and leave. I'm a busy man."

"I've made my decision. You can end the trials and start making arrangements for the wedding. I'll be marrying Victoria Hamilton."

At first, my father doesn't say anything. He just continues drinking his wine in a cold and calculating way.

"Do you know what I did last night after that stupid girl decided to decorate my hall with her brains? I went out and organized the final task. I want this over, and it won't be until the tasks are done. Elizabeth Sandford undertook hers a few hours ago and succeeded. We have a nice, new Picasso to hang up on the wall. A stupid private collector was insufficient with his security. She was good. I'll have to show you the video at some point." He places his glass down. I can feel the hairs on the back of my neck start to rise. I don't like this one bit. There's something not right.

"At the time, I couldn't find Miss Hamilton, no doubt, because she was sitting on your dick somewhere."

"She's pure," I lie through my teeth. I won't have him disregard her and seek to destroy her this way.

"Yes, about as pure Charles II favorite, Nell Gwynn, was." He waves his hand toward a stolen painting of the famed courtesan on the wall. "Anyway, it was fortunate that you chose to phone your butler this morning. I've had a trace on your phone since the day you got it."

The blood must drain from my face because my head starts to spin.

"What've you done?"

"At this very moment, I suspect that Miss Hamilton is

being taken from your mother's summer house — it's a good place to go, by the way, and proves you're as weak as she was. Miss Hamilton will be put in location to steal her painting within the hour."

I don't wait to hear anything else from him. I'm out of the room, out of the house, and running across the grounds as fast as I can to the summer house. I leap over the formal gardens, filled with summer blooms and edged with boxed dark green yew. A water fountain has me skidding in a different direction, but, eventually, I burst in through the doors of the summer house.

"Victoria?" I call, but the only answer I get is Reggie, falling to the ground in front of me. "Reggie." I leap forward and pull him into my arms. He's holding a wound to his chest.

"I tried.," he splutters, and blood drips from his mouth. "I'm sorry they took her."

"Shush," I urge him and press my hand against what looks like a knife wound in his chest. "I need to get you a doctor."

"No," he gurgles. "Too late."

"It can't be." I'm shaking my head. Reggie has been the father I've never had. He's looked after me for as long as I can remember. "Let me try?" I'm pleading with him. I can't lose him.

"I'm old. She's young. Help her." He coughs again, and his eyes roll back in his head.

"Reggie." I shake him, but there's nothing to be done. The room goes silent as he passes away. I lay him down on the floor. I can't breathe. This wasn't supposed to happen. I was supposed to go to my father and be marrying Victoria. Victoria, she's got to steal. I need to think. We have a list of works that we want. Which one would it be? Oh god, the ultimate prize. Would my father send her after that? The Mona Lisa. I have to hope that he has some sort of heart amongst the ego that dominates his body. I spin around, ready to finish this, but my father stands in the door, a tablet in hand, and a microphone headset on.

"One less expense on my budget, then." He looks over my shoulder to where my butler lays dead.

"I want the guard who killed him. I'm going to tear him apart, limb by limb."

"So dramatic." My father rolls his eyes

"Reggie wasn't just staff. He's been more of a father figure in my life than you've ever been"

"Well that explains the weakness in you, then. He always did pander to your whims when I thought you should be beaten black and blue, to instill some balls into you. I should've had someone stick a knife in his chest years ago."

"Give me the guard," I repeat.

You've more important things to worry about than the staff." He hands me the tablet.

"What's this?"

"I thought you would like to watch the woman you love."

I swipe the screen quickly, and it brings Victoria up. She's in a dimly lit room, but I can make out her silhouette.

"Miss Hamilton" –my father addresses her, and she jumps– "I trust you had a good evening with my son. I know you were expecting him to come back and whisk you away into a happy ever after, but I'm afraid I can't allow that to happen. I don't believe you'd be the best choice for Duchess of Oakfield. You're what I'd call 'a little too headstrong'. Alas, I have to go through the rules, and you must be given a chance."

"Fuck you," Victoria shouts out into the darkness, and I smirk at her bravery.

"I don't do sloppy seconds, Miss Hamilton. I'm afraid you are spoiled goods, now. When I prove it, I'll have you executed for your disregard of the rules, but, for now, this is much more fun."

"Let her go!" I snarl at my father.

"Nicholas?" Victoria must hear my voice.

"I'm here."

"Don't give into his demands. Remember, I'm stronger than I look."

I smile because I have a feeling that my father is the one who's doing the underestimating of the situation, when it comes to Victoria.

"I won't."

"Hush," my father snaps. "Miss Hamilton, you have half an hour to retrieve a painting from the vault you are in. If you fail to do it in that time, then you're at the mercy of the collector. I'd wish you good luck, but I'd be lying. Your time starts now."

My father takes the headset off his head and throws it on the floor. I stare down at the screen, and the lights come on. I don't recognize where she is but breathe a sigh of relief as I know it's not The Louvre, in Paris. The Mona Lisa isn't the picture she'll seek.

"Victoria isn't headstrong. She'll make a good Duchess of Oakfield."

"She'll destroy the rules, and the society will be left penniless."

"Is that such a bad thing?" I ask. "Haven't enough people died?"

My father yawns. "You've become such a bore. That's why I've had to do things this way. You gave me no choice. It's your mother's fault. She put weak genes in William, and they seem to have gone in you as well."

The door behind him creeks, and Elizabeth Sandford appears in the doorway.

"Your Grace, she drapes her arm around my father. He greets her with a kiss on the cheek and pats her stomach.

Oh, Fuck!

"There's only one way that this will end, Nicholas, and it won't be with you marrying Victoria. You'll marry Elizabeth and claim my son as your own. You'll then disappear, taking the bitch with you if she survives, and you still want her. I don't care. You'll leave me with the title until my, sorry, your son comes of age. I'll do this again. This time correctly and without your mother's weakness. Elizabeth Sandford is perfect for the mother of a Duke."

"Go to hell." I spit at them both. "Elizabeth Sandford is a title grabbing bitch. She'd just as soon stab me in the back as she would you."

Elizabeth smirks but doesn't deny the accusation.

"And that's why I trust her better than anyone. She's a devil, just like me. She's what you should be. We'll raise a boy together who'll make this society the greatest it's ever been. We'll eclipse the royal family for whom the society was originally designed, to provide them with our support. We'll become the royal family. Everyone will bow to us. Worship us. We'll be gods.

"You're delusional and will be thrown into a mental asylum."

My father laughs.

"Actually, maybe I should have you declared insane, instead of making you disappear. That would be fun."

"Please, stop now. This is no longer your decision to make," I plead with my father. I'm pretty sure I'm wasting my breath, though, especially when he stabs a pudgy finger at the screen of the tablet that I'm holding.

"You'll do this, Nicholas, or she'll die in that room. There'll be no way out with the picture that she's stealing."

"No."

Elizabeth kisses my father's cheek.

"I'm glad I chose the father over the son. He's a fool."

"He is, and one who's about to watch the woman he loves die."

CHAPTER TWENTY-SIX

VICTORIA

I squint as the artificial lights turn on and flood into my sensitive eyes. It takes me a few seconds to adjust to my surroundings, and what I have to do. The society, or rather the incumbent Duke of Oakfield, wants me to steal a painting, and he's talking to me through an earpiece. My heart beats fast. I can't do this. I'm not a thief and wouldn't have the first clue on how to steal a painting and get away with it. I could stand there and appreciate the brushstrokes for hours, but other than that, I'm probably screwed.

The world comes into focus and my breath hitches. I know exactly where I am. I'm back in my home, well, in the vaults underneath, which my father uses for a safe. It dawns on me what's going on, and just what picture I need to steal. When I first became interested in art, my father took me to a sale at Sotheby's in London. I fell in love with the place and the notion that decent paintings could be sold in this manner. Up until that point, all of the art that I'd researched was primarily on the walls of museums. We'd walked around for hours looking at the pictures, but every time I came back to the same one. A Van Gogh painting of roses. It wasn't a prestigious one in the art world, but I fell in love with it. When the auction started, I stood in shock and watched as my father bought it for me. I can't remember the exact price, but it was a lot of money. At the time, I thought I was a fortunate girl and had a father who worshipped me. I know better, now. My father doesn't have much other valuable artwork, mostly paintings of ancestors by obscure artists from the time, but the Van Gogh will be the one I'm here to steal. Oh, the irony, I have to take a painting that already belongs to me. I should call out for my father and demand he opens the safe, so I can walk out of here with it. But I suspect that's not the game the Duke of Oakfield wants to play.

I shut my eyes and try to think back about the security system my father has. I know it's state of the art because the vaults contain family jewels worth a lot more than the painting. Lasers are protecting the area around the safe, and there's a code to get into it. I know the code by heart. It's the date that he made his debut for the English polo team. He was a phenomenal player in his youth — he still is. Shame I'll never get to see it again, not that I want to. I grind my teeth together in anger. When I get out of this, I'm going to talk to Nicholas about confronting my father and making him pay. Hell hath no fury like a woman scorned, and my daddy will reap what he sowed. But for now, I need to figure out how I can get past these lasers, which, should I touch one, will lock down the room and call security guards to arrest me.

Thankfully, the Duke dressed me appropriately. I've got a black cat suit on. It's all very Catherine Zeta-Jones in the film where she tried to steal artwork. I'm pretty confident that to be a member of this society, which Nicholas will one day rule, you have to think with your dick, not your brain. It must be in the initiation process — if you can pass a math's test you are out, but if you can drool over a topless woman and masturbate in a room full of strangers, then you're a candidate for membership. My temper is rising. I want to damn them all to hell, but for now, I have to play the game. Thankfully, I've done Yoga and Pilates ever since I can remember —

I'm flexible and have good balance. I get down on the floor. The first laser beam — I know it to be about hip height. I slide under it and over to the left, as the next beam dissects from a ninety-degree angle to the right. I get to my feet and step over the third, which is only ankle height but awkward because another beam comes straight down to it from the roof. I have to press myself against the wall to pass it.

I stop to get my breath. I don't know how, maybe it's because the Duke is twisted, but I know Nicholas is watching me. I can sense it in my body. I duck under a head height beam. My back still aches a little from the beating I received, and I'm a bit stiff from my exploits with Nicholas last night, but I'm determined to do this, to show the Duke he'll not win. I have three beams left. I shut my eyes and picture them. One on my left dissected by a waist height barrier and the last one coming down from the right. I can't help it — my hands start to shake. My father always said that his guards will ask questions, only, after they shoot whoever tries to steal from his vaults. I have to get this right, or I could gain yet more wounds, which might not heal as well as the physical and emotional ones that I already have. I take a deep breath and maneuver my body through the last three lasers. I make it. I want to jump and shout but decide on quiet being the better course of action. With shaking fingers, I enter the code into the safe door, and it opens. I'm so nervous that a fine layer of sweat has appeared on my body, and the sound of my teeth chattering together, fills the room. I inch into the room and past my family heirlooms. I'm tempted to take them with me to spite my father, but that would only hurt my brother in the long run. God, I hope that Theo doesn't know about the society. I don't think I could bear knowing that he's a part of it. I continue past the jewelry to where the picture is hung on the wall. I take both sides of it.

"Is this what you want, Your Grace? You going to put it in pride of place next to the stolen poppy picture? or with some of your other ill-gotten gains?"

Laughter echoes in my ear.

"I see my son is a talker during sex."

"No, not during. He's just got manners and talks to a lady after he's fucked her into oblivion. Mind you, I believe you just fuck a lady into a hospital." I'm finished with the politeness. "I've done what you've asked. I have the picture — now, get me out of here and let me see Nicholas. Your time as the Duke is over, retire quietly, and I'm sure we won't destroy everything you've worked for."

"You don't have the picture, yet," he retorts with a gravelly malevolence.

I pull the picture off the wall, and an alarm sounds.

Shit!

I've messed up badly. I forgot the hidden wire over the front of the picture. The vault door slams shut. I drop the picture to the floor and wait for my death.

CHAPTER TWENTY-SEVEN

NICHOLAS

"Victoria," I call out at the screen when the piercing alarms start to sound. "What's happening?" I step closer to my father with my fists balled, but he stands there unaffected and continuing his eerie laughing.

"She was so close but allowed her temper to get the better of her and messed up. Now, she dies."

I lose it and grab him by the throat, pinning him against the wall.

"Put a stop to this now."

"Henry," Elizabeth screams and tries to pull me off, but she has no hope. I'll have blood on my hands in a minute, unless my father calls off the guards.

"You know my terms, Nicholas. You want me to put a stop to this then you marry Elizabeth and disappear never to be seen again," he spits into my face.

"I want William," I counter.

"He stays here. I'll not have him embarrassing my name with his weirdness."

"He's not weird — he's autistic."

"He's as crazy as his mother was. Now, make a decision. Tick-tock, tick-tock."

I push off the wall and stamp across the room and send my fist flying into the stone wall. I come off worse with what, I suspect, might be broken knuckles.

"Fuck!" I call.

"Tick-tock," my father repeats.

"Fine. Stop this. I'll marry Elizabeth." I turn back and slump down the wall. "Just save her."

My father presses a button on his tablet and struts across the room to throw it at me. I pick it up and see a figure, in the society's livery, flash across the screen. One minute, Victoria is there, and the next, she's gone. A few seconds later, a hail of bullets flood into the room and destroy the painting.

"She'll be kept in a safe place until you have upheld your part in this bargain. You'll prepare to leave at once. We travel to Scotland tonight. You'll be married by the morning. Say goodbye to Oakfield."

With those words, he leaves. I stare at the bullet-ridden painting. I wanted to save Victoria, marry her, and destroy the society, which has governed both our lives since the day we were born, but I've failed.

CHAPTER TWENTY-EIGHT

VICTORIA

I'm thrown into a dimly lit room by the man who swept me off my feet from my father's vault. The door shuts, and a key turns in the lock. I scramble to my feet and try the handle, but to no avail, I'm locked in.

"Where's Nicholas?" I shout but get no response. "Let me out!"

Nothing.

I kick the door — however, given that it's solid oak, it hurts my foot more than it makes any damage, which could be used as a means of escape.

"Fuck, fuck, fuck." I jump around holding my sore toe. "Nicholas," I try again. What the hell is going on? I look around the room that I'm in and realize that it's my bedroom at Oakfield hall. The secret passages! I run across the room at a hobbling pace but don't make it to the door before it opens, and William appears. I fling myself into his arms.

"Oh, thank god. We have to go. You know these passages. We've got to get out of here. I need to find Nicholas."

I pull back and look up at him. He's pale, and he opens and shuts his mouth like a fish, looking for words.

"William. What is it?" My heart sinks.

"Words. They're funny. Normally, I have loads of them." He flicks his hand over his hair a few times. His other hand is against the wall and tapping repeatedly. "I can't find them."

"William. Is Nicholas alright?" He's scaring me. I'm fearing the worst, and my legs feel like they're sinking to the floor in defeat.

"He's gone."

"Dead?" I whisper, my voice breaking.

William shakes his head rapidly in the negative, and I suck in a breath of relief.

"Words, William, find them," he chastises himself.

"It's alright. I'm here." I hold the hand that isn't tapping.

"I wanted my brain to work properly, so I could be good enough to save him. He and you could run away. I'll be what the Duke wants, but I was made wrong. Miswired and a freak."

"Hush. There's nothing wrong with you. I need you to calm down, though, and tell me what's going on. Come sit on the bed." I lead the man who's almost the spitting image of his older brother, except for a bit paler, over to the bed. I settle him down, take hold of his hand, and allow him to tap his comforting rhythm onto my leg.

"Nicholas has gone." William won't make eye contact with me. It's a sign of his condition but also a result of his agitation.

"You said he's alive? Where's he gone?"

"Scotland."

"Scotland?" I question.

"To marry."

"Marry," I repeat with dumbfounded shock.

"He chose Elizabeth as his wife — she's pregnant."

The walls I've built around me, to stay sharp, tumble down. I stand up and pace. My head is suddenly all over the place, fearing the worst.

"Elizabeth's pregnant."

"The Duke wants them married as soon as possible." William still can't look at me. This time, though, I know it's because of the shame that he's feeling for his brother's actions.

"Elizabeth's pregnant," I repeat, and tears start to fall from my eyes. I've been played by the society again. Now, I see it was all a game. Nicholas is no different than his father. He warned me he was the devil, and I chose not to listen. I allowed myself to fall in love with him. I'm the biggest idiot on the planet. He was after whomever he could get pregnant first. He never had any intention of changing.

I look at William. He's tapping a rhythm on the bed. Is it all an act with him as well? The whole fucking family played me. They've no respect for women. It's all one big game to them.

"Get out!" I shout at him. He looks up and shakes his head.

"No."

"Get out." I step toward him and slap him hard on the face. "I hate you all. I'm sick of being a pawn in your twisted games. Go!"

"Victoria?" he stammers.

"Get out," I scream and cover my ears, so I can't hear any more of his lies. I screw my eyes shut, not wanting the reminder of my mistakes and foolishness in front of me, anymore. "I just want to go home. This is over. Nicholas has made his choice. Just let me go."

I open my eyes and see William is by the door to the secret passageway in my room. He shakes his head.

"William?" Something's wrong — I can sense it.

"I'm sorry. When you're told that 'you're nothing', you believe it. I wish I could help you, but I'm not strong enough. I don't know how to." He turns quickly and disappears into the passageway. The door closes behind him, and I hear it lock. No. That door is always open. Why is he locking it? I pull on the handle, but it doesn't budge.

"William," I call with trepidation but receive no response.

"Argh!" I pull on the door, once more, then turn and run back to the main bedroom door. I tug on that, but it's still locked. I ball my fists up and hammer hard against the oak. It hurts like hell, but I don't care. I want out of this room.

"I want to go home," I shout. "I've failed your stupid tasks. Nicholas has chosen his Duchess. Let me go. Let me fucking go!"

A laugh, I would recognize anywhere, comes from the other side of the door. I stop hammering and step back.

The door opens, and two guards flank either side of the Duke of Oakfield as he enters.

"Miss Hamilton, I see you've learned of my son's betrayal. Women are such weak creatures — easily convinced that they're in love, and so they drop their knickers. Whores! The lot of you." I step forward to slap him, but one of the guards grabs my wrist and pushes me against the wall. My face is slammed against the velvet lining of an ostentatious wallpaper that depicts the society's crest. The guard moves to one side and allows the Duke to press himself, and an erection, against the seam of my ass. I try to fight, but I'm not able to move.

"My son's made his decision. You're not under his protection anymore. If I want you strapped to the bed and to fuck you till you bleed all over my dick, then I can. But you're tainted, and I'm bored of your mouth."

"Fuck you." I spit behind me, and it hits him square in the jaw. He thrusts harder against me.

"Mind you, I can always change my mind." He lowers his hand over the clothed curves of my body until his fingers rest at the cleft between my thighs. I want to be sick. The cat suit is thin in texture, and I can feel his dirty nails digging into my sensitive flesh. He swirls a finger around my clit. I'm dry to his touch. I'll never feel pleasure from a man's touch again. "Alas," he continues his speech, "I have a wedding to get to. The future of the Oakfield line is assured. You thought Amelia would be the last to die for our name, but you were wrong. *Ultra Vires*, we're beyond their power. Nobody will ever stop us, and more will die for our pleasure. Women are nothing — they are weak and feeble. A womb to raise our sons. Not that, *that* will be your future." He rubs himself harder against me.

"Enjoy your last few hours of life, Victoria Hamilton, for by sunrise you'll be dead."

"Let me go," I whimper and plead on a sob.

"You know too much," he snarls.

"I'll never talk."

"Never leave a loose end."

He steps back and pulls me with him. I fly across the room and smack into the wall on the other side. My ribs hit a brass hanging, and I collapse with the pain.

"You really thought you'd beat me. I'm the fucking Duke of Oakfield. I'm the ruler of this goddamn society. My word is law." The Duke stalks after me, shouting his diatribe. I'm on the verge of blacking out.

"One day, you'll be stopped. I might not have been strong enough, but there'll be more women like me. One day, whether it be thirty years or three hundred years, a woman will be strong enough to stop this. Your name and legacy will be destroyed.

The Duke kicks me right in my ribs, and I can't keep the shriek of agony inside me.

"I'll be dead and buried, by then. I really don't care. All I care about is now. Goodbye, Miss Hamilton. I wish I could say it's been a pleasure knowing you. Actually, no, it has. I've enjoyed defeating someone who thought they could match me. You've made this whole process much more interesting. I'll take that knowledge into my retirement and use it as fire when I fuck."

He strides to the door. I try to crawl after him, but

I'm in too much pain.

"Until we meet again, in hell." He stops at the door and smiles. Then, he turns to one of his guards.

"Place the call to Laird McGuire — tell him I've got a pretty little toy for him to break."

My stomach lurches, and I vomit on the floor.

CHAPTER TWENTY-NINE

NICHOLAS

As I stride through the corridors of my father's dominating castle in Scotland, Elizabeth Sandford tries to slide her arm into mine. I'm still covered in Reggie's blood, and his death hangs heavily on my shoulders. I wasn't able to arrange a burial for him, before I left. My father told me he'd deal with it, but I fear my beloved butler won't rest in peace until I can figure a way out of this.

"I'm feeling a little dizzy. Can we walk a little slower?" Elizabeth interjects into my thoughts. "It's been difficult to eat the last few days."

"Shouldn't have gotten pregnant with my father's spawn, then," I snap.

"Nicholas, this makes sense. Don't fight it. We all get what we want."

I grind to a halt and stare at her.

"Are you actually for real?"

"What?" she pouts.

"I've never met someone so greedy in all my life. This has only ever been about the title for you. You'll let my father do anything to you, as long as you have the prestige of our position. You're sick."

"No." She stomps her foot. "I'm not the sick one. Victoria's right. Your society members are the insane ones. What makes you in charge of us? My father has worked hard and has nothing. He listens to all the crap you, and everyone else, spout. Just because he's a Bishop, you all think he's not worth your respect. Your father's the only one who's ever listened to him. Well, I'm going to show everyone you're all wrong. It's you, and your little boy scouts group, that's worthless."

"You're deluded." I shake my head. Elizabeth knows full well the reputation that her father has amongst the choir boys, and that's why he gets no respect from us.

"We'll see about that." She pats her stomach.

"Is it even my father's? You know he'll demand DNA testing."

She steps forward and slaps my face. I crack my jaw because it's one of those blows from a woman that ricochets right through you.

"You ever raise your hand to me again, and I'll become the devil everyone wants me to be. I feel absolutely nothing for you but contempt. I wouldn't normally hit a lady. But in your case, I'm willing to make an exception because, well, the term 'lady' only loosely applies." She goes to hit me again, but I grab her hand, swing her around, and dump her on the floor.

"Your father will hear about this."

"Tell him — I no longer care," I spit out at her before trudging off to my room and slamming the door like a petulant teenager. I need Victoria — I've not spoken to her since she was rescued from the failed painting theft. I don't trust my father, and the fact that he travelled after us leaves me suspicious. I pull out my phone and message William.

Nicholas: Hey, have you seen Victoria?

I look at the icon on the screen where the three dots appear. They flash for a few minutes then stop. I get impatient. Eventually, a reply comes through.

William: Yes. Not that you deserve to know.
Nicholas: What's that supposed to mean?

William: You married yet?

I'm getting the distinct impression that my brother's pissed off at me.

Nicholas: Still working on getting out of it.
William: Don't lie. The Duke told me everything.

I stare down at his message. What the hell does he mean?

Nicholas: I'm not marrying Elizabeth out of choice. I agreed to it under duress. I'm doing it because it's the only way to save Victoria's life. I saw the trial — she was about to die. Once the marriage is done, Victoria and I will disappear. The baby isn't mine, before you ask. I've never slept with Elizabeth, so it can't be. It's our father's.

I hesitate before sending that message. My father won't let me take William with me, but I'll never stop trying. I add a little bit on the end.

Nicholas: As soon as I can come back for you, I will. I'll never stop trying.

The dots appear again.

William: You love her?
Nicholas: With all my heart.

I wait a few minutes, but nothing comes back. I put my phone down on the dresser and head toward the bed. I need a shower — I've been in the same clothes for days. Removing my jacket, I place it into the linen basket for cleaning. My heart pangs for Reggie. This would have been his responsibility. I'm defeated and can take no more. I sit on the bed, place my head in my hands, and exhale deeply. I don't know how to win this game that I find myself in. I feel as though I'm drowning. I've been an arrogant sod most of my life: spoken down to people beneath me, fucked anything with a willing pussy, but Victoria Hamilton has floored me with her spirit. I'm not sure that I can continue with my life the way it is. I don't want to marry Elizabeth Sandford, nor do I trust my father that this will all end, now. I flop back onto the bed, allowing my eyes to shut. I need sleep. Hopefully, once I've had some, I'll be able to comprehend my situation better and deal with it. A rap at the door destroys my plans, though.

"Enter," I call and pray it isn't Elizabeth Sandford come back for round two. I exhale a long sigh of relief when I see it's a uniformed servant.

"I'm sorry to disturb you, My Lord." He seems nervous, and his soft Scottish accent's tinged with trembles of worry.

"What is it?" I grumble.

"I have something for you. It's" –he stutters– "it's a letter."

"From whom?" I don't even bother to sit up on the bed. I lay my head back and close my eyes.

"Your mother." That brings me upright.

"What?" I demand. "If this is some kind of joke, I'll have you castrated."

"It isn't, My Lord. You have my word. I knew your mother well. I tried to help her and make her life easier, but I met her after it was too late. Her mind had already gone. She didn't deserve what happened to her..." He pauses. "It's not my place to say, but I don't believe she took her own life. Your father..." He stops. "I speak too freely. I'm sorry." He reaches into his pocket and pulls out a letter. "Shortly after you were born, she gave me this. It's always been the tradition to come here for the wedding, and she asked me to give it to you before yours."

I shuffle from the bed and stare at the man in front of me. I'm trying to size him up. He seems genuine, but I've been fooled already by my father, and I don't want to fall into his trap again.

"Why should I believe you?" I ask.

"You don't have to believe me. I'm just doing what I promised your mother." He drops the letter onto the dresser. "You have her eyes, and the sparkle behind them that I watched die. Read the letter, My Lord. Don't let your light die." With those words, he disappears from my room, not waiting to be granted permission to leave. I look down at the letter like it will bite me. My name is written on the front, and it seems like my mother's handwriting. I've seen it often enough in her diary. I reluctantly reach out and open it. There's a single sheet of paper inside, and what looks like a much older letter. I read the newer one first.

Dear Nicholas,

My handsome son,

If you're reading this, then I'm dead, and you're about to be married. I can pray until I'm blue in the face that it's to a woman you've fallen in love with, via conventional means, but I know your father too well. Your marriage will come as a result of the Society's rules placed upon you. Your bride will have gone through tasks, unimaginable to others, to finally be chosen. The girls who have failed will be lying in barely cold graves.

I've known, since the moment I looked into your blue eyes for the first time, that you'd be the one to end this nightmare. I saw more compassion and kindness in the eyes of a mere, few moments old, baby than I had seen my entire life. I knew then you were special, and I had to protect you as best I could. When William was born, I saw the same unique qualities in him. Despite the dark blood that runs through your father's sovereignty, you'd both inherited mine. My pure and gentle abilities. I spent all the time I could with you both — Firstly, in the hope I could keep it hidden from your father, and secondly, to stop him from beating it out of you. I took the blame for misdemeanors. I hid your brother's eccentricities. I prayed as hard as I could you would stay strong. Your father hated me for it. I don't like to speak evil of the man who's half of you, but I can't find a good word for him. He's the devil, my son. I've seen the things he's done to people, not just women. He's a tyrant and a dictator with delusions of grandeur. I'm sorry if this hurts you. I wish there were some other way. I know he's your father. The night I conceived you was shortly after our wedding. I'd been a virgin until that night, and I'll never forget how brutally my innocence was stolen. I'd not healed, physically or mentally. Your father became angry when the doctors stated I needed another week's rest before he could resume his activities with me. As always, he chose to ignore them. I was stripped by my guards and brought naked through the house to him. He was already in bed with another woman. I remember the fear in her eyes as I came in and was introduced as his wife. I don't know the story that he'd spun her about our relationship, but I could tell she wasn't willingly in his bed. She was chained, her lip was split, her eye black from bruising, and his rough marks had already left blemishes on her body. He started to penetrate her from behind, and she screamed so loudly. Then silence. An overwhelming and deafening silence. He had a knife hidden under his pillow and had slit her throat. She'd have seen her death coming but couldn't have prevented it. I mourn her every day, especially after what happened next. Your father withdrew from her and grabbed me around the neck. He shouted at me for being unready for him. He blamed it on me that he'd needed to treat the woman in that way. I had tears streaming down my eyes. He called me weak and useless and said that it wasn't the doctors' decision to make, regarding how he treated his wife. After that, he bent me over the bed, I looked at the dead girl, and we conceived you. I was bedridden for months after. They were terrified that I'd lose you due to the damage I had suffered. I'm sorry, my son, to tell you this. I've only ever wanted you to think that you were conceived from love, but I can't. I can't lie if it means that you remain ignorant of the truth about what your father and this society are. They're evil men, and you aren't. You're the one who can put a stop to this.

Contained within my letter is another. It's from the first Duchess of Oakfield who was submitted to the trials. There's a prophecy that one day a boy will be born who'll end this. He'll be pure of heart and able to cast off the evil of the legacy of his succession. The letter, it states, will only come to light when that boy is born. It's you, Nicholas...you're the child. I found it shortly after you were born. It proves you're better than this. It demonstrates that you can put an end to the suffering of the women who have followed my fate. Utilize the strength that I know is in you and stop the society. Don't let them win. If you truly love the woman you're due to marry, then go ahead with it and make her your wife, but if there's any doubt in your mind then end it here. Please, please my son, don't let another generation suffer. Have courage, I'm with you always in spirit and know that I'd never leave you unless it was through no choice of my own.

I love you,
Your mother.
The Duchess of Oakfield.

I take a stumbling step back onto the floor. My legs won't hold me. To read of her suffering, during a time which should have been romantic and filled with love, brings tears that tumble in rivulets down my cheeks. 'Grown men don't cry', my father would say to me. But I'm not weeping for myself, I'm mourning for the woman who nurtured me within her for nine months despite being broken and destroyed. I wipe away tears for a mother who fought hard to give me compassion and love when she was shown none for herself. She was an angel the day she was born into this society, and now she's an angel in heaven, giving me the strength I need to end this.

I take up the other letter and carefully open it — it must be over four hundred years old.

To whomever reads this,

My name is Alice, Duchess of Oakfield. I'm the first Duchess to be chosen under the rules of the Oakfield Society. But, I hereby declare that they are false and should have no future bearing on the generations to come. The rules are governed by men who were intent on the destruction of my husband. You see, you cannot choose to marry when you are already wed. The Duke and I were married before the trials began. I wasn't a virgin going into them, and I carried his child after the third trial. They were a sham, and the only reason I went through with them was to protect my husband's place in the society and to save his life. I loved him, and I couldn't lose him. The Oakfield's have a great name, an honest and trustworthy one, or so it was once, before the society's rules. Whichever future Duchess discovers this letter will be the mother of the son who is destined to return our name to greatness. We shall once again be the Oakfield's of my husband's previous generations, and the legacy will finally be forgotten.

I'm sorry for my part in the terrible pain that others have experienced. I was weak and blinded by the love I felt. I hope one day I shall be forgiven.

Alice, Duchess of Oakfield

I can't believe what I'm reading. I've spent years thinking that this was forced upon women, but the first Duchess chose her fate, misguided through love or otherwise, and sealed it for future generations to come.

The anger grows within me. This letter was from a woman four hundred years ago — my fate, and the fate of the generations before me, has been determined because of her decision. It ends now, though. Enough!

I jump to my feet and am at my bedroom door in seconds. I pull it open and jump back when my father stands there with a gun. The man who delivered the letter to me lays at his feet — dead I assume.

"Your mother always did like to interfere where it wasn't needed. It's why I had to throw her off the roof of Oakfield Hall."

I growl my livid response and leap at him just as the gun goes off. Pain rips through my right shoulder, and I slump back against the wall.

"And this is why I've planned your succession the way I have. It's all been a game from day one. Elizabeth knew she would be Duchess from birth. I only needed you present for the wedding to take place. Thankfully, Elizabeth's father is a very helpful Bishop."

My father looms over me, as I slide down the doorway. I'm trying to focus on him, but the world's spinning and darkening.

"You were never destined to become the Duke of Oakfield. I was always going to be the one to take it on for another thirty years."

He kicks me in the shoulder, and I grunt in pain.

"Your destiny was to die."

CHAPTER THIRTY

VICTORIA

"Get off me, you bastard," I scream and thrash out as I'm dragged, unceremoniously, down the hallway by a guard. I don't want to die at the hands of Laird McGuire, and I'm going to do everything in my power to prevent it. I bite the hand of the guard, and he slaps me. It's a sad state of affairs — but, I'm so used to being a punching bag that I don't even react to it. We reach a closed door, and I can hear the Scottish Laird on the phone in his room. Even his voice sends shivers through me. Any pretense I had of trying to escape leaves me, and I sag into the guard's arms.

He knocks on the door and opens it when addressed to do so.

"I've got your present from the Duke, Laird McGuire."

I shudder when the brutish Scotsman looks me up and down then licks his lips. He's dressed in a plaid kilt with a white shirt and black waistcoat. He looks every inch the gentleman, but I know better.

"A very bonny lass indeed, ye must thank His Lordship for me."

"Where would you like her?" the guard asks.

"On the table, please. I've got cuffs for her hands 'n' feet. Ensure they're done up tight. Don't worry about removing her clothes. It's a part o' my fun." His face lights up in an evil grin, and as I'm taken across the room and laid out on the table, I watch him pull a bag from under his bed. The guard ensures that I'm securely fastened before standing back. He too looks smug and self-assured. At this very moment, I want to wipe the smirk off both their faces, but the fear has taken hold of me. Nicholas has broken me — the Duke has helped him. I thought myself in love. I gave my body to a man who played it like a musical instrument and wrote a symphony with my heart. Like many classical masterpieces, though, it will end in a violent crescendo of haunting melodies. An epitaph to the torture I'm about to experience.

"Ye can go," the Laird informs the guard, and the man sullenly leaves. "I'm going to do this in privacy."

I know he wants me to fight him, speak back, and enrage him into hurting me further, but I've lost my fight. I just want it over with and to be dead, hopefully in heaven.

"Let's get ye out of those clothes."

The ginger-bearded Scotsman pulls a large knife from his bag and comes to the table. I'm still wearing my catsuit. It's easy for him to cut away in seconds, leaving me in only my bra and panties.

"Such a bonny little thing. What to do first?" He brings the point of the knife down to my belly button and trails it up toward my breasts. A red line of blood follows behind it. He doesn't cut me open, but he marks the skin enough to cause me to bleed. He tucks the knife under my bra and pulls the blade up. It cuts the flimsy fabric in half and exposes my breasts to him.

"It's a shame they are na bigger. A like something, I can get my face lost in. A woman's tits are like honey to a man like me." He bends over and wraps his hair-lined lips around my nipple. I squirm away from his touch. Big mistake.

"Ye think ye can escape yer fate." He laughs and punches me straight in the stomach. I want to curl up, but I can't with my hands and feet tied. "I'm going to suck these tits until they're raw. Then I'm going to remove yer pants and stick my dick in that tight little cunt off yours for the next few hours. Don't get over excited about it, though, because I want ye dry as a bone. I'll rip ye apart — much better that way. Ye are going scream my name in so much pain that everyone in the place will know exactly what I'm doing to ye. Once I'm bored of yer pussy, I'll be going for yer asshole. A can be fuckin' all night, but if my dick gets tired, I have toys. Toys designed to tear ye so wide ye'll be begging for death. Once done with the fucking, the good part starts." He punches me again in the stomach and steps back toward his bag. He drops the knife into it and pulls a gun out instead. I will him to pull the trigger and end my suffering, but he's not done tormenting me...yet. No, he comes back over to me and trails the gun through the line of blood that he's left on my stomach. This time, he heads toward the lower half of my body. My legs are parted by the cuffs, and he places the gun at my entrance. I let out a small whimper...I can't help it. The smile of satisfaction on his face makes me sick. I shut my eyes. "The only way a whore like ye should die. Shot in the fuckin' cunt. Enjoy yer last few hours, Victoria Hamilton, because I'm going make them hell."

BANG!

The sound echoes in my head. Pain. I should feel pain. I must be dead. He shot me. A heavyweight lands on me, and a breath is forced out of me. I open my eyes, and the Laird is laying over me with a hole in the back of his head. I panic. I'm pulling the chains but can't get free.

"Stay still." William appears in my line of vision. A still smoking gun in his hand. He places it down and pushes the Laird off me before undoing the cuffs. I scramble up, off the table, and across the room away from the dead body. My stomach heaves, but I haven't eaten or drunk all day and nothing comes up.

"I need to get you out of this room." William comes up to me with a blanket. "Let me put this around you." I can't breathe. I should be dead. I don't want to be rescued. I want to go to heaven and find peace from this constant pain in my chest. I can't do this anymore. I want the torture to stop.

"Why did you stop him?" I push William away.

"It's ok. Let's go to a different room, and I'll explain."

I start crying, all the emotions flooding out of me. Over William's shoulder, I see the gun lying on the table. I can end this myself. I speed past him before he realizes what's going on. I pick the weapon up and hold it to my head.

"Goodbye." He turns to face me, and I pull the trigger, but nothing happens.

"I only had one bullet." He looks sheepish. "I didn't really think about what I'd do if I missed the Laird."

My situation is so utterly hopeless that I burst into laughter. Fate's conspiring against me, I can't even end my life or the suffering I'm under.

William dares to come closer to me. He places the blanket around my shoulders and brings me to his chest. He smells like Nicholas.

"We have to go to Scotland." He strokes my hair.

"Why?" I ask — my whole body is feeling weak and deflated.

"Nicholas was tricked by my father."

"I don't understand." I suddenly find firm feet and plant them securely enough to allow me to look up at the younger Cavendish brother.

"Nicholas doesn't want to marry Elizabeth. He's in love with you. The baby isn't his either. He's never slept with Elizabeth. It's our father's."

"I don't understand. Why's he marrying her then?"

"The Duke made him watch you, during your trial.

When you went wrong, and your father's security were coming, he agreed to marry Elizabeth, so my father would save you."

I gasp and reach behind me to steady myself on the table that I was strapped to, moments ago. "He loves me."

"Yes."

"Your father's been playing games with us all along."

William nods.

"I think he still is. Nicholas said to me that once he's done what the Duke wants and married Elizabeth, then our father will allow you and him to disappear." My friend swipes at his worry spot on his face —it's something I've come to recognize as a part of him.

"But the fact that the Duke handed me to Laird McGuire for sport and execution suggests otherwise. He's going to kill him."

William turns pale, but I spring into action. I push past him again and head for the door.

"Where are you going?" he asks.

I turn back to him.

"Well, firstly I'm going to get some clothes on. Then secondly, I'm going to Scotland. I'm going to rescue the man I love and, hopefully, kill the bad guy."

CHAPTER THIRTY-ONE

NICHOLAS

The murmur of voices wakes me, and the memory of being shot by my father floods back. I try to move, but I'm too weak — my shoulder hurts like a mother fucker.

"He's waking." A feminine voice enters my head, and I realize it's that bitch, Elizabeth Sandford.

"About fucking time," my father broods. "You, on your feet and get on with this wedding."

That brings me to my senses. Wedding! I open my eyes and see my father standing next to Elizabeth's father, Hubert Sandford, The Lord Bishop of Monchelsea, and is dressed in his full regalia. Hell no!

The Bishop starts to speak.

"In the presence of God, Father, Son and Holy Spirit, we have come together to witness the marriage of Nicholas Cavendish, Earl Lullington and The Honorable Elizabeth Sandford, to pray for God's blessing on them, to share their joy, and celebrate their love."

"Bullshit!" I interrupt.

"It's not. It's our wedding vows," Elizabeth counters. "Daddy, tell him."

"I...er," the Bishop stutters.

"I agree, it's bullshit," my father adds. "Just get to the part where he has to sign the register — then, I can end his miserable life.

"I thought you would at least make this special for me," Elizabeth whines.

"I'll make things special for you later." My father winks at her.

"I have to at least make some attempt at the vows,"

Hubert Sandford intervenes with a green color flushing around his gills.

My father snorts.

"I don't think you do. I've got a present for you outside, which suggests otherwise. One that I know you'll be very interested in."

The Bishop takes the register and signs his name on it. Elizabeth stomps forward and does the same, with a sullen expression on her face.

"You better do whatever I want tonight, my love." She kisses my father on the cheek and hands him the pen.

"You seem to forget who's in charge here, Elizabeth. You do whatever I want, or despite my feelings for you, once that baby is born, you might find yourself the unhappy victim of an accident. I did it to his insane mother. I'll do it to you as well — if you destroy my love for you with defiance."

"I can't believe you can say such hurtful things," she whimpers on the verge of tears.

I laugh.

"What?" She stamps her foot.

"My father loves himself, nobody else. I'm his flesh and blood, and he's going to kill me. You're nothing but a willing vagina to him. I did try to tell you. Shame you'll have to learn the hard way."

"Shut up, Nicholas," my father commands.

"Tell me that isn't true." Elizabeth throws herself at my father, and he glares at me over her shoulder.

"I'm just trying to make a better life for the two of us and our son. You knew I was a bastard when you fell in love with me. Don't expect me to change. I'll protect you with everything I have but defy me, in any way, and I'll cut you down."

Elizabeth sniffs back her tears. My head spins, and I'm not sure if it's the excruciating pain in my shoulder, or the sickening display in front of me. Part of me actually feels sorry for Elizabeth, only a tiny portion though. She's brought this on herself by being a bitch.

"I only meant that maybe I could go on top tonight. I like the way it feels."

My father pulls back and strokes her hair. "As long as I get to see those tits bounce, I don't care what position you're in, on my dick."

I make a gagging noise.

"Seriously, you're going to buy that? And you..." I look at Elizabeth's father. "You're going to let him speak to your daughter like that in front of us. I mean, have you no shame?"

"If your father has outside, what I think he does, then no, I have no shame. I'm giving my daughter to your father in exchange for rewards beyond your comprehension. He can have carnal relations with her in whatever way he wants," the Bishop retorts.

I shake my head.

"Victoria was right. Everyone in this god damn society is an imbecile." I've been sitting on the floor, against a wall, throughout this entire conversation. No doubt, this was where my father had his guards dump me. I push up to a standing position, but I'm dizzy due to blood loss from the gunshot wound. I rest against the table on which lies the register that requires my signature to seal the fake marriage.

"Sign the paper, Nicholas. Let's just get on with the inevitable. I'm bored of the conversations. I've got plans for this society, and I've had to wait far too long to implement them."

I stare him down with utter contempt.

"You've been in charge for almost thirty years. Why didn't you take on the world during that time? Why do you need my thirty?"

My father turns to the Bishop.

"If I just chop his hand off and sign his name with it, does that count? Does he really have to sign the register himself?"

"For it to be valid, yes. I can't in all conscience lie to God about marriage." The Bishop makes the sign of a cross on his chest and bows his head.

"Yet, you can rape a little boy," my father angrily replies.

"Some things can be overlooked." The Bishop pushes the papers toward me.

"You're sick." I snarl at him.

"Sign the papers, Nicholas." My father steps up behind me, and the next thing I know, I'm falling to the floor in the throes of torment. My father has his finger stuck into my wound. He's tearing the flesh farther away from the bone and rupturing more blood vessels to allow claret liquid to seep from the bullet hole. I should be stronger than him — under normal circumstances, I would be, but he's rendered me into a small boy again, begging at his feet for mercy from punishment. I thought I deserved it, then, but now I know what a demented bully my father is.

"Go to hell!" I scream.

He digs deeper, and my head swims with dizziness.

"You think you've got something to live for?" my father asks, and my mind goes to Victoria. No, what has he done to her?

"Where is she?" I ask.

"Right now?" he laughs.

"Probably flat on her back with Laird McGuire's dick in her cunt or ass."

I shriek in anguish and beads of sweat start forming all over my body.

"Seems I found a use for the Scots in the society, after all. I bet he's tearing her apart. I almost wish I could've stayed in London to hear the bitch scream. I bet it'll be loud. The very foundations of Oakfield Hall will be shaking with what he's doing to her."

"You bastard."

My father removes his finger from my wound. I breathe rapidly, trying to get through the pain and anguish that I'm feeling. Victoria will be dying in a torturous way, and there's nothing I can do to save her.

"I'll ask you one last time. Sign the papers." I roll onto my back, and my father places his foot on my chest.

I waiver. What have I got to live for? I've been an arrogant, rich brat all my life. The only good thing to ever happen to me was Victoria, and I'm the reason she's going to die. I shut my eyes again, waiting for the inevitable.

"You might as well kill me because I'm not going to sign them. I'll never make it easy for you to take over the society for another thirty years. I want to destroy it. Let's hope my death does that."

Silence. Nothing. I open my eyes again just as my father brings his boot down toward my face.

"I wouldn't do that if I were you." A dreamy feminine voice floods my senses, this time. It sounds like an angel. Victoria, my Victoria. I must've gone to heaven. But, no, I'm still on the floor of a room in a castle in Scotland. My father lowers his foot, and we all turn to the door. Victoria stands there next to William — both have guns pointed at us. They're dressed in jeans and sweatshirts, and both look ready for a fight. I'm not sure what I'm more shocked at: Victoria being alive, or the fact my brother has left Oakfield Hall, for the first time ever.

"I'm afraid Laird McGuire couldn't uphold his end of whatever bargain you made with him. He came down with an unfortunate case of a hole in the head. Couldn't happen to a nicer man, if you ask me," Victoria continues cockily.

"Did my other son finally grow a set of balls?" My father steps forward, but William cocks the gun.

"I wouldn't if I were you, Father." The last word is spat with venom. "I don't like the future you have planned for Nicholas and Victoria very much, and I've found that years of playing shooting games on consoles has left me with an excellent aim."

"You would kill your own father?" The Duke raises a skeptical eyebrow, and I use his, momentarily, distracted gaze to shuffle to the side of the room. I need to regain my senses if I'm to help my brother and Victoria. Neither one is strong enough to survive the evil that could take place here.

"I've had enough of your games and self-righteous nature. You've no right to treat people the way you have. No bit of paper can decide my fate, only I can do that. The society ends here and now." Victoria meets my father halfway across the room. William remains at the door with his gun aimed at the un-moving Bishop and Elizabeth.

"So confident, yet I see the shaking in your hands. Tell me, how far did the Laird get before William saved you?"

Victoria smirks when she responds, "Not far enough to break me."

"Damn," the Duke replies unhappily.

"Why can't you just accept he doesn't want you and fuck off to hell." Elizabeth steps forward this time and wraps her arm round my father's.

"Are you talking about the Duke or the Earl, Elizabeth, because I'm pretty sure I would pass on the former."

"The Earl got me pregnant, you stupid bitch. He's a cheater and a liar."

"No." Victoria maintains her poise and calm so gracefully that, despite the situation, I can feel myself getting hard in my pants. "The Duke got you pregnant when you opened your legs for him for a title. I'm guessing that, as Nicholas is most definitely the better looking of the two, you slipped into a little fantasy world at some point and imagined it was the Earl. I know he wouldn't touch you with his dick even if it was on fire and needed a wet place to extinguish it." Victoria raises an eyebrow at the end of her retort, and I let out a little chuckle.

"Are you going to let her speak to me like that? Kill her," Elizabeth demands of my father.

"She's the one with the gun. I'm afraid there isn't much that I can do." My father edges closer to Victoria. I'm wary of the action.

"But you've got your own gun in your suit jacket," Elizabeth replies.

Everything happens in slow motion. My father growls and pulls his own weapon out. He fires at the same time as Victoria does. Thankfully, his shot skims past and into the wall behind. I turn to follow the path of Victoria's bullet just as I watch it slice through Elizabeth's chest. My father is behind her — he'd pulled her in front of him. Elizabeth gurgles blood from her mouth as the life drains from her. My father lets her slip to the floor. Victoria stands shocked at what she's done, and it's just the advantage my father needs. He grabs her and pulls the gun from her trembling hands and drops it to the floor. I'm on my feet as quickly as my blood loss allows me. William's rushing forward at the same time, but we're too late. My father has Victoria around the throat, and a gun pointed at her head. We both skid to a halt.

"My daughter." The Bishop falls to the floor and begins last rites.

"I've failed you, Father," Elizabeth speaks through struggled breaths

"No!" her father cries.

"I only wanted to make them see you're a good man. It's all you've ever taught me."

"I know, my child, I know."

Elizabeth tries to speak again, but only her final breath of life comes. She slumps lifelessly into her father's arms.

"You promised me that she wouldn't be hurt." Hubert Sandford's mask of piety slips. "I'll make you suffer for this."

Without even batting an eyelid, my father removes the gun from Victoria's head and shoots the grieving man between the eyes.

Victoria screams as he slumps forward in a heap on top of his daughter.

"Couldn't have happened to a nicer man," my father jests.

"How about you point the gun at yourself?" I counter and take a step closer.

"Uh, uh. No. You stay just where you are. I'm not a fool. Here's what happens. If you want Victoria alive, then I suggest you both move out of my way. I'm going to take her with me as collateral for a while. It seems that I need to think of another plan."

"Not going to happen. You're going to put the gun down. We still have a weapon trained on you."

"Yes, by the most stupid man in London."

"I'm not stupid — I'm autistic," William shouts.

"Same thing." My father rolls his eyes.

"You've no idea about either of your sons, do you? Who we actually are? Autism hasn't made me stupid. It's given me the ability to focus. I can do things with a computer nobody else can. If you'd actually bothered to be a father to me, then you could've used my skills to further your stealing of artwork. But no, I wasn't normal, so you disregarded me. And as for Nicholas, you've no idea what sort of man he is. You think he's the arrogant bastard you've made him, and in some ways he is, but he's a born leader with it. He'll take the society into the future and make it great. You'll just run it into the ground and have everyone, who doesn't agree with you, arrested or shot." William's foot taps the entire time he speaks. I can tell he's stressed beyond words, but he's maintaining his composure, thanks to his tics.

"I don't believe any of that for a moment. You're both weak and feeble, just like your mother. Her genes have spoiled you both."

"No." It's my turn to step up to the fight. "Her genes have made us the good men we are, despite the malevolence from you that runs through our veins. Enough games — you know that you won't get out of here with Victoria. Let her go."

Victoria's watching me get closer and closer. Her eyes flick to the wound in my shoulder and anguish fills them.

"I'm walking out of here," my father reiterates.

"And we'll let you — just not with Victoria."

"What do you see in her anyway? Elizabeth was the prettier of the two. She's got no discernible features as far as I can tell. How can you let her ruin what we could do for this society? Isn't there a part of you that wants more? We could rule the country together, you and me."

"Victoria has everything. She's beautiful, compassionate, and fiery. She's made me see that there's more to power than being a dictator. Plus, if you'd actually taken time to know her as a woman, not an object, you would've seen she probably knows as much about the art world as we do. Maybe even more." With every word I speak, I'm edging closer to where my father holds Victoria around the neck. He pulls the gun away and points it at me.

"Stay back."

It's the chance I need. With the gun pointed away from Victoria, I'm close enough to leap at him. Despite the pain from my wound, I take him by surprise and punch him in the face. Reeling, he lets Victoria go, and she scrambles away. I need to disarm my father before he has a chance to fire off the gun again. I ignore the fiery spasms shooting through my body and wrestle him to the ground. I release his hold on the weapon, and I push it away. Now, we're even.

"Give up Father. I'll give you your life and a pension to live quietly somewhere, but this is over now."

"Never. You weren't born to lead." He punches me in the shoulder, and I cry out, swearing I see stars.

Then, we're on the floor and rolling over. I'm on my back when my father brings another blow down on my shoulder. If I have much more of this, I know I'll pass out. That's the last thing I want.

"William, do something." I hear Victoria say.

"I…I…I…," he stutters back.

I bring my good arm around and catch my father on the side of the jaw. He wavers a little but doesn't fall.

"Why couldn't you have just loved us?" I shout.

"Because he doesn't have a heart." I hear William shout — his voice filled with anguish.

A gunshot goes off, and my father's body goes lifeless on top of me. William appears and pulls my father off me. Then disappears to the side of the room to tap out a rhythm. I notice the back of my father's skull is missing, and my head swims with nausea. I don't have a chance to retch, though, as Victoria slams her body onto the floor next to me and brings her lips to mine.

"I thought I'd lost you."

"I love you. Everything he said was lies. I didn't want to marry her. I want you."

"I know. I know." She kisses me again through her

tears, which fall freely. I reach up and touch one.

"No more tears." She's cradling me in her arms, and I can feel the dark clouds looming again. I look toward William, and she follows my gaze. "Look after him for me."

"What?" she stammers. "No, Nicholas."

I don't hear anything else for the world goes black.

VICTORIA

"How long is this thing supposed to take?" I look toward my best friend Tamara while she sits on the bed swinging her legs.

"It says five minutes."

"That's far too long." I pull on the ends of my vibrant red hair, due to nerves.

"You've got five minutes to spare. Remember the thing about having a whole life ahead of you." She tuts at me.

"That might be about to change."

It's been a month since the day the old Duke of Oakfield died, much has happened in the interim. I'm not sure that I've processed it all yet. Nicholas was rushed from the castle in Scotland to a hospital with barely even a faint pulse. William and I sat by his bedside for three long days before he woke. He'd lost so much blood that his body had started to shut down. The doctors had given him a transfusion and put him into an induced coma to recover. I don't know what happened with the Duke, the Bishop, and Elizabeth Sandford's bodies. William disappeared for a while and told me that he'd had someone deal with it all. There'd be no repercussions for anyone. I think it was at this point that I realized just how far above the law the Dukedom of Oakfield is. William had retreated into himself after that. It had taken so much courage for him to leave his home in London. I could tell that all the people who came and went from his brother's bedside disturbed him. I told him he could return home if he wanted to, but he refused. I didn't know what was going on in his head although I feared it wasn't good. He'd killed his own father to save his brother, in addition to his years of anguish and repression. None of that could be erased quickly or easily.

Eventually, Nicholas woke, and we rejoiced. The doctors said there should be no lasting issues with his shoulder, but it would take a while to heal. He'd need physical therapy to rebuild his strength. Nicholas, being the stubborn man he is, told them he'd be fine. Then he promptly spilled the cup of tea they'd given him everywhere, when he tried to lift it with the damaged arm. It was at that point I took control and told him he'd follow the doctor's orders, or I'd have him strapped to the bed until he agreed. He seemed to like that suggestion far too much because he then promptly called for a priest — we said our vows and consummated our marriage that same day. It wasn't how I pictured my wedding day, but when I told Tamara about it later, I was sobbing with the beauty of it all. That is what has led me to my current predicament — Tamara and I staring at a little stick I've just peed on. I'm unsure how I feel about the result.

I am the Duchess of Oakfield. I shouldn't worry about being pregnant as my future is secure. It's more Nicholas' reaction I'm scared off. This is all still so new for both of us, and the stigma of how we fell in love surrounds us daily. The former Duke's reaping his own type of torment, even from the grave. Why give us contraceptive injections at all if they were going to be fake? Yes, placebos apparently, another ploy by the Duke to mess with our heads. It was the one piece of information I was able to get out of Doctor Fallen before I told him that he'd better disappear because if Nicholas found him, he'd be dead.

A loud bang on the door makes me jump. The door

handle rattles. Tamara gasps and shoves the pregnancy test under my pillow.

"Victoria, why is your door locked?" Nicholas shouts from the other side. "It's my right as your husband to get into this room whenever I want."

"He sounds furious," Tamara whispers.

"He's just being Nicholas," I reply and sweep off the bed toward the door. He bangs again before I can turn the key in the lock.

"Open up, now!"

I unlock the door as it almost comes flying off its hinges with the force of his entrance.

"Why was it locked?" he growls and stalks toward me. Nicholas will always be Nicholas. He has an arrogant and bossy side to him, but I love it because it's counteracted by the softer side he keeps hidden only for William and I. The younger Cavendish brother follows the elder into the room, and I wave at him.

"Me, focus on me," Nicholas moans.

"Yes, husband," I counter with a twist of my lips.

"Why was your door locked? Mrs. McDonald said you didn't eat breakfast this morning. What's wrong? Who do I need to threaten to fix it?"

I look over at Tamara — William has come to sit next to her on my bed. They smile at each other, and I swear I see Tamara's cheeks blush. She refocuses her attention on my warring husband, and I shrug.

"Sit down before you hurt yourself," I direct Nicholas toward a chair. He reluctantly sits. He's still wearing his arm in a sling, to allow the wound to heal.

"Victoria, talk to me." His voice softens — I can see the worry in his eyes. I perch on the side of the chair.

"It would seem that the contraceptive injection Dr. Fallen gave me was a placebo."

"What?" his face whitens.

"You know that we've barely left the bedroom since

you were discharged from the hospital. Well, it seems that every time we've had sex, we've been doing it without protection."

"You're pregnant?" he questions.

"I don't know for certain." I look to Tamara, and she pulls the stick out from under my pillow and waves it in the air. "The door was locked because we're doing a test."

"You haven't read the answer?" Nicholas asks.

"I have to wait five minutes."

"Have the five minutes finished?"

An alarm goes off on Tamara's phone. William quickly picks it up and silences it. He doesn't like loud noises.

"What does it say?" Nicholas demands of Tamara.

She gets up off the bed and comes over to us. William follows.

"I think this is something you two best do alone." She hands me the stick face down. "William, I've been hearing about all this great artwork that you have here and how it's going to be sent back. I'd like to see it before it goes. Would you show me?" She holds her hand out for William. He looks down at it.

"Is that the hand that just touched the pee stick?"

Tamara laughs, steps up behind him, and pushes him toward the door.

"Come on, I promise I'll wash my hands before we touch the pictures."

They both leave, and I'm left alone with my husband. Both of us looking at the stick in my hand like it's some kind of poisonous instrument of torture.

"Are you scared?" Nicholas asks me.

"No, I'm not, actually. If I'm pregnant, I know that you and I will be the best parents we can be to the baby."

"Even with my past?"

"Because of your past." I shuffle so that I'm straddling him on the seat. I feel his cock go hard underneath me.

"I love you," Nicholas offers me with genuine warmth and affection.

"I love you, too," I respond. "On the count of three."

He looks towards the stick.

"One, two, three."

I turn it over, and the words, 'You're pregnant' are on the little screen.

"Well, it looks like we're having a little Earl or Countess Lullington." He smiles up and me and brings his lips to meet mine.

"You're happy?" I ask.

"I couldn't be happier. A whole new start. I know we've still got a lot to sort out with the society. So many people, including your father and Lady Joanna Nethercutt, have gone to ground. We need to find them and prevent what happened to us from happening again. We've given our dead the burials they deserve, be they innocent or a villain of the peace." My mind flicks back to the day of Reggie's funeral. I thought he was just a butler to Nicholas, but I saw my husband break down that day. He was an emotional wreck and has still to employ another butler to replace his friend. Nicholas told me, the evening of the funeral, how Reggie had been like a father to him over the years. He'd been there for so many of his firsts in life. His father had never done that. Speaking of his father, that funeral couldn't have been more different. It was only Nicholas, William, and I in attendance, and I solely went with Nicholas to support him. There were no feelings of loss that day, only remorse that their father was so self-absorbed that he was unable to see them both for the great men that they'd become. I didn't cry when they lowered the Duke's coffin into the Earth, No, I rejoiced quietly. I felt nothing but pure hatred for the body that was being given to the worms for dinner. No one mourned the loss of the old Duke of Oakfield.

Nicholas' good hand has been on my backside supporting my weight on his lap, but he removes it and reaches into his jacket pocket. He pulls out papers. "I was going to give these to you later, but now seems a good time as any. The society and the title were all in my name, but I had my lawyer make everything fifty-fifty. All decisions on its future will be made jointly."

I take the papers from him. My heart falling even more in love with the man in front of me if that was possible.

"You didn't have to do that."

"It'll take me a long time to trust that I have a good nature. I've done bad things. I've been a bastard for so much of my life, but I know with your guiding voice I'll be alright. This is my way of ensuring that, together, we rule. *Simul ut praeesset*. I'm changing the motto to reflect the way we're going to be working."

I drop the papers to the floor behind me and lean into my husband.

"I want you inside me."

"I want to be inside you." He gives me a lustful smirk, and we make short work of divesting only the clothes that are hindering our desire to be joined. I don't need foreplay, not today. I've been wet since Nicholas walked into the room. I always am around him. I slide myself down onto his erect length until he fills me. The sensation is overwhelming and captures my breath every time. Two people, as in love as we are, joining as one in this most intimate of ways. Nicholas places his hand on my hip and helps guide me up and down his cock. I'm breathless already with the fire burning brightly in my core. I've suffered. I'm not the precious little princess I was a few months ago. I've learned about life, discovered about love, and you know, I wouldn't change a thing that happened. Well, maybe I would have kept my mouth shut, so I didn't have to experience the scold's bridle.

Nicholas' thrusts get faster and faster. I meet him with every one. The urgency between us is frantic. I smash my lips against his and come with a call of passion while I shudder feverishly around his dick. His own climax hits him. I feel his cum flood my body and combine with my essence as it has done before when it formed the baby that now grows in my womb.

I slump down onto Nicholas' chest, and he uses his good arm to bring me closer to him. I know he has no plans on pulling out of me anytime soon. We will sit like this for as long as we can.

"I always thought the legacy of my succession would be the same as my forefathers," he speaks. "But no one counted on you being born into the society. The prophecy spoke of a boy to end the suffering, but in reality, a woman has been stronger. We are going to re-write all the rulebooks. A new legacy starts today."

THE END

The Dark Sovereignty Series continues with

TAINTED REASONING

Coming 4th December 2018.

William and Tamara's story.

Coming 4th December 2018.
William and Tamara's story.

"Why would I let the world see him? He's imperfect. No, he needs to stick to the shadows where he'll not bring shame to this family."

William Cavendish thinks he was made wrong. The autism, which causes his brain to function differently from what's typical, has been a thing of scorn all his life. With his father's death and his brother taking over the Oakfield title, William is discovering that he can have the life he dreamed off, maybe even love.

Tamara Bennett recently finished her lawyer's degree and is using the knowledge that she has to help her friend, the Duchess of Oakfield, bring down a dark society that has tortured women for years. Is it a case too big for the fledgling lawyer?

Tainted Reasoning is book two in the Dark Sovereignty series. It tells a story of discovering who you are and what you are capable of when needed.

Let's build a better world together
rather than just extinguish the fires of hate.
~ Dark Sovereignty Series by Anna Edwards

THE CONTROL SERIES

The Control Series: A dramatic, witty, and sensual suspense romance set predominantly in London.

Surrendered Control

Divided Control

Misguided Control

Controlling Darkness

Controlling Heritage

Controlling Disgrace

Controlling Past, The Control Series, Book 7:
Coming 2nd October 2018

Amy

Amy emerged from the water to the full moonlight glistening over the endless volcanic sand. The bright illumination shone on her honey-blonde hair, and she brushed her fingers through it to separate the wet strands. The day of travelling had left her tired, and the warm water eased her aching muscles that had been cramped by the budget flight. This was her first holiday in many years because aspiring writers didn't tend to have the money to travel. Nor dancers in a gentlemen's club, forced to work just to make ends meet. But it wasn't as bad a job as it sounded because she was well protected. Her uncle ran it and made sure she was sheltered from the seedier side of the profession. She enjoyed the dancing side; it was her second passion after writing. Her uncle, Stephen, paid for this holiday to Lanzarote as a twenty-first birthday present. Ever since her parents died in a car crash two years ago, he'd looked out for her. He was the only family she had left, and she respected him and trusted him implicitly.

She took a towel and wrapped it around her body, the aroma of the freshly caught fish being cooked in town was everywhere and made her mouth water in anticipation. She decided on a small tavern, which was filled with more locals than tourists. She wasn't big on the mass-market tourism of the island and preferred places of culture and history, but as the holiday was a gift, she couldn't refuse it. She ordered the grilled catch of the day with salad and a glass of the local *La Geria* wine. As she watched the sun slowly set over the shimmering waves, the tension in her shoulders began to dissipate.

When she finished her delicious meal, Amy ordered another glass of wine and pulled out a little notebook from her bag to begin writing down some of the details of the island so far. She liked to bring her personal experiences into her writing, and she wanted to get everything noted should it be needed for future stories.

She'd just finished a passage on the chaotic wait for her luggage at the airport when an uneasy tingling warmed her skin as though she were being watched. Looking up, she met the alluring sky-blue eyes of a man sitting across the room. Had he just arrived? Or how had she not noticed him previously? He too was sitting alone with a glass of wine for company. Upon making eye-contact, she couldn't help but blush. He was exquisitely handsome. He'd a rugged, yet, smart look, a defined jaw line, and short dark hair, which he ran his fingers through as he watched her. The top few buttons of his blue linen shirt were undone and revealed a muscular upper body, which oozed a primal masculinity. His stare was intense, and she felt herself being drawn into it even more. When his lip twitched at her blatantly checking him out, she pushed the other chair at her table out with her gladiator-sandaled foot and looked up, smiling at him with a cheeky grin, which masked her excitement. For a moment, she thought he wasn't going to move, but then, he got to his feet. Even the way he walked was sexy. She was glad she was sitting down as her legs felt like jelly at his presence. He took a seat and held his hand up to the waiter, who promptly took his order for a more expensive bottle of wine. Neither of them spoke at first. They continued to take each other in.

"James." His voice was deep and inviting, and she was

pleased to note he was speaking English.

"Amy." Her voice was smooth and possibly a little bit too sexy when she spoke.

Silence.

"Well, if this isn't awkward." He ruffled his hands through his hair again. The bottle of wine arrived, and the waiter poured them each a glass.

"Shall we start again? I'm Amy. I'm twenty-one. I come from London, and this is my first holiday in a while. I've come away to finish writing my first novel."

"I'm James. I'm twenty-eight. I also come from London, well Kent initially. I haven't had a holiday myself for a while. I tend to be a workaholic."

"What do you do?"

"I work in property. It's all very boring, I'm sure you don't want to hear about it. So, a novel? Is it all hush-hush, or can you tell me something about it?" He sat back in the chair, his left leg resting over his right, the wine glass tantalisingly resting at his full lips. Lips that she couldn't tear her eyes away from. She wondered what they'd taste of, if she kissed him? He seemed happier to be asking questions than answering them, so she decided to answer him to continue that line of conversation.

She chuckled and took a mouthful of her wine. "It's a classic boy meets girl, boy loses the girl, boy wins the girl back forever."

"Interesting. So, this boy? What's he like?"

"Tall, dark, and handsome."

James nodded with genuine interest.

"And the girl?"

"Pretty, slim."

"Blonde?"

"Blonde."

"I like this story already."

"Told you it was a classic."

"Certainly is." He raised his eyebrow as he spoke. "So, is the man proficient in the bedroom?"

"That's a little presumptuous isn't it?"

"Why?" He chuckled, as he refilled the glasses they both seemed to have drunk rather quickly.

"They've only just met."

He shrugged, "Why should they waste time, if there's an attraction between them?" James reached forward, took her hand, and their eyes met in an intense stare, as sparks of electricity flowed through them both. She wasn't drunk, so it wasn't that. "Are you staying nearby?"

The question hung thickly in the air between them.

She'd had only one previous partner, and that was a boyfriend of four years. Strange as it seemed, she felt she knew James, which was odd since they'd only set eyes on each other not fifteen minutes before. "Yes, the Rivera apartments."

"Do you want me to walk you home?"

She didn't doubt from the look on his face that this would turn to sex if he did. But something about him, something about the mystery of his tone prevented her from saying no. He had a presence about him that drew her under his spell.

"Yes."

James pulled out his wallet and put forty euros on the table. The walk back was short, and they talked a little more. Just general facts, where they grew up, favourite foods, drinks, and a particularly funny story about an encounter that he'd had with a flock of seagulls in Brighton. She didn't tell him she worked in a Gentleman's Club.

When they entered her apartment, she was suddenly nervous. James took a seat on the cream sofa, and she went to look in the kitchen for a drink. She found two glasses and a semi-chilled bottle of wine and returned to the lounge. His big body was so commanding in the small lounge.

"Sorry, it isn't more. I only arrived today."

"It's fine. I still haven't bought any wine for my apartment, so you're a step ahead of me."

"How long have you been here?"

"A week now. A few days left. How long are you here?"

"Only a week."

"Not long to finish that novel then."

"No. Not really. I'll have to forgo sunbathing and do lots of writing."

She put the bottle down on the table because she needed a corkscrew to open it. "I won't be a minute. Just have to figure out which drawer the corkscrew is in." She turned back to walk into the kitchen but stopped as James called out 'wait'. It was the way he said it—it sent shivers of anticipation down her spine. Slowly, she turned and looked at him, her eyes wide. He'd risen from the sofa and was walking towards her.

"Take your dress off."

"I...."

"Take your dress off."

She had no answer. Her mind was telling her this was crazy, but her body was doing as he asked, completely disobeying the part that was telling her to tell him to fuck off. She reached down to the hem of her dress and pulled it over her head. She wasn't big breasted, so underneath the summer dress, she hadn't worn a bra. She stood in front of him in a pair of white lace panties. He walked around her, studying her, taking in every inch of her prickling flesh. She could feel the heat of his gaze marking her. She was never *naked* in front of the clients at the club, but she wore revealing clothing, and none of that could prepare her for what she was feeling right now. He leaned over her and took a deep breath, he was smelling her.

"You're beautiful." His tone was calm but had a stern undercurrent to it.

"I was supposed to be getting you wine."

He laughed. "I'm going to kiss you now. Are you sure you want to do this?"

"I don't think I'd be standing in front of you in my panties if I didn't. Now, are you going to remove some of your clothing?"

"Eager. I like it. But we will do this my way." James pulled his shirt over his head, and she noted she was indeed correct about his superbly toned chest. She couldn't see his back, but she saw on his left arm he'd a tattoo. It looked like the tips of wings.

"What's your tattoo?"

His face went momentarily blank. He didn't answer but pressed his body closer to hers. He leaned in and kissed her. Tender at first, and then with intense passion. She could feel her knees weakening as she was pushed back against the wall. "Place your hands above you head and don't move them." Again with the authoritative tone.

"Why?"

"Will you do as I asked? Or should I leave now? I told you; we will do this my way. You'll enjoy it. Don't worry." A hot kiss was again pressed to her lips and without thinking anymore, she moved her hands above her head. "Good girl. You'll be rewarded for that later."

Rewarded? James moved his mouth from her lips down to the peaking tips of her nipples. His tongue swirled around the sensitive buds, and she let out a yearning moan. He looked up at her, a mischievous look in his eyes, and began to travel down the flat line of her stomach until he knelt on the floor in front of her. He placed his hands on either side of her panties, and in one fluid motion, ripped them from her body. She was breathing fast, now. This whole experience was so damn intense it almost seemed like a dream. Her body was on fire, and she longed for him to touch her.

James put his hands between her legs and parted them to reveal her neatly trimmed sex. He groaned. "I haven't even touched you, yet, and you're ready for me. Have you been like this all night? I can even smell your arousal."

She sure as hell wasn't going to let him know that he was turning her on more than she ever had been before. "You know how to kiss a lady and get her excited. It's a good start but depends on what skills you have now."

He gave her a little tap on the top of her thigh, which brought a scream from her, and then ran a finger over her displayed folds before moving it slowly into her inner channel.

"If you doubt my skills again, I'll put you over my knee." Her body writhed against his hand and she found herself being excited about having her bottom spanked.

Holy hell. Where had that come from?

His thumb found the hidden bundle of nerves between her thighs and teased it. She could feel the heat within her starting to build. "If you don't stop doing that, I'm going to come all over your hand." James abruptly withdrew his finger and got to his feet with a tutting sound.

"No. Not yet. You'll come when I tell you that you can." He looked her in the eyes, and it was almost like he was controlling her body with his words.

"You're not in charge of me, you know that right?"

He didn't answer, only sniggered, reached into the pocket of his trousers, brought out his wallet, and retrieved a condom from it. The wallet was then tossed aside, and she watched him lower his trousers and pants to reveal a substantially thick cock and covered it with the condom. It was jutting up towards his stomach and was a work of art. It should be framed and hung in an art gallery. It was that perfect. She was panting, now. Although, she was terrified that the length and girth of his manhood was going to hurt, but at the same time, she needed him buried deeply inside her. *Now!* She wanted to know what he felt like. She pulled her hands down and reached out to touch the muscular sinews of James's shoulders.

"No. You don't touch me, unless I give you permission." He slammed her hands back against the wall and held them there with one hand. With the other, he lifted her leg from the floor and in one slow thrust pushed inside her.

"Oh God," She groaned. He was nothing like she'd felt before. Her ex-boyfriend wasn't small, but sex between them had always been something that they seemed to do, because they were boyfriend and girlfriend. This was different. It was raw, and it was dangerous. James began to move slowly. Their eyes locked together as with each long movement he stroked against the sweet spot deep within her.

Their lips joined in a tango of passion. His hand still held her in place, and she was glad for it because she was barely able to support her weight. She felt the build-up of her climax again. She tried to suppress the feeling. James had told her that she couldn't come until he gave her permission, and she wanted to please him.

Jesus, what was this man doing to her? This was her body. Why was it responding to his control like this?

He seemed to know she was close and trying to control herself; she could tell by the little curl of his lip. She wanted to hit him. She wished he'd let her release. He finally let her out of her misery when he leaned forward and collected her lip between his teeth. He nodded consent, and she exploded around him. Wave after wave of cataclysmic pleasure rolled over her shaking body. She called out, and he joined her over the precipice as he released himself into her.

They were both covered in sweat; breathing rapidly, their legs quivering. James lowered her leg to the floor and withdrew from her checking the filled condom.

"Are you alright? I didn't hurt you, did I?" She shook her head. She couldn't find her voice just yet. "Good." He pressed another kiss to her now-bruised lips and looked into her eyes. At that moment, something within him changed. She saw it. Gone was the dominantly splendid lover he'd been; he withdrew into himself. He pulled up his trousers, quickly found his shirt, and put it on. "I'm sorry. I shouldn't have done that." And with that, he left her confused, standing naked, covered with the scent of the best sex she'd ever had, and her hands still above her head.

GLACIAL BLOOD SERIES

The Glacial Blood world is full of intrigue, suspense, and kick ass fights. It also features a secret that should remain untold. A family isn't always blood — it's the people in your life who accept you for what you are.

The Touch of Snow

Fighting the Lies

Fallen for Shame

Shattered Fears, The Glacial Blood Series, Book 4:
Coming 31st July 2018 – Pre-order now for $1.99

The barren desert wasteland with its hues of gold, orange, and red sped past the car window. The rock formations were a testament to years of erosion, beaten down by forces greater than he could understand. As a shape-shifting snow leopard, Brayden Dillon knew a lot about the ways of Mother Nature. Considering he spent most of his time exploring the snow-capped peaks of The Glacial National Park he already had the air-conditioning turned up as high as it would go. The brand-new Ford Mustang he drove had been a gift from his alpha, Kas, in recognition for a job done well; so was the break from duties as pack Enforcer. Why his mother had to live just outside Death Valley was beyond him. You really couldn't get a hotter place on Earth. She'd told him it was because his father had always lived in the snow. When he died, she decided to get some sun. She hadn't looked back.

He pulled his Mustang up outside the café and shut off the roar of the high-powered engine. The disapproving looks from the locals soon vanished when he climbed out of the car. His height of six foot five silenced any potential disagreement. He purred to himself in contentment, but that was quickly lost when the heat of the midday sun hit him. He was not designed for this weather. He had all the usual snow leopard attributes: thick black hair with smoky gray flecks, small ears, and big feet that helped with balance. He was pale because he rarely spent time sunbathing like the lions and tigers in his pack. Dusk to dawn was when he was the most active. He made quick steps towards the café and into the air-conditioned building.

He didn't see his mother, only a fresh-faced waitress. She wore the café's uniform: a barely-there skirt and a tank top that was almost a second skin. She was pretty, in a timid sort of way. Every time someone came near her she flinched, and he could smell her fear. Well, he assumed it was fear. His judgment was slightly clouded by the fact that he needed a drink, preferably ice cold and dumped over his head. She approached the seat he had taken near the counter.

"Hi. Welcome to the Last Stop. I'm Selene, and I'll be your waitress today. Can I get you an ice water to start with? It sure is a hot one out there today." Any sign of her nerves had disappeared, replaced with a business-like smile.

"Yes please, lots of ice. In fact, just bring me a big bowl of ice."

She laughed, her tiny nose crinkling up and dimples appearing in her cheeks. Up close, she was even prettier than he'd originally thought. "Let me guess." She took a step back and looked him up and down. "Well, the fact you seem as if you're melting, I take it you're not a southerner. The lack of a tan confirms that but I can't quite place the accent?"

"Montana."

"No wonder you're hot. I'll bring you ice cream as well." She spun around in her little ballet pumps and started to stride off. Something stopped her. She turned back and took another long look at him; an eyebrow raising in question.

"Brayden?"

"Yes." His reply was tentative. Not many people knew who he was. It was his job to be secretive and stay in the shadows.

"Your mother said you were coming. She had to go to a meeting in Pahrump. She should be back soon, but she said that you could go up to the apartment if you wanted. My God, now I really look at you, you look like the pictures she has of your father. God rest his soul." She bowed her head. Brayden couldn't help feel a little unease. This girl, she couldn't have been more than eighteen from the looks of her, knew far too much about him. He just hoped she didn't know everything. His mother would never tell her that, would she? "You head on up. I'll get your water, ice cubes, and ice cream, and bring it to you. It's my lunch break, I'll keep you company till she gets here."

He did as instructed. Mainly because he was freaked out by the insistent waitress, but also because his mother had the biggest freezer known to man. If he didn't get cold air on him soon, he was going to dissolve into a pile of fur on the floor.

His mother's apartment hadn't changed one bit from when he visited last year. It was decorated in a minimal style with clean lines and equally clean surfaces. She had always liked the latest trends in interior design. It had apparently annoyed his father, to no end, because he preferred to take things as they came, which, in his case was usually wild and chaotic. While he waited for Selene, Brayden opened the freezer and stuck his head in it. The blast of icy, cold air surrounded him, and his inner beast jumped for joy at finally getting away from the inferno that was the Mojave Desert. It was definitely scolding him for coming to this place. He'd introduce it to a snack of jackrabbit later. That would keep it happy.

"Damn, you are hot." Selene's voice came from the doorway. How had he not heard her? She blushed. "I mean..."

"I know what you meant. I spend a lot of my time in the mountains in Montana. I'm more acclimatized to snow." He watched her while she placed the food on the table.

"Come on and sit down before the ice cream melts.

You look like a cookies n' cream guy. I hope you like it. I'll turn up the AC."

"I can do it."

Surprised, she dodged out of his way when they both reached for the air-conditioning remote control. It was such a quick movement, almost cat-like.

"Please sit. I've already got it."

He took a seat at the table and downed the glass of ice-water in one mouthful. Its cold liquid reduced his body temperature. Selene pressed a button on the remote control, and another icy blast hit him. He purred, as he finally felt relaxed with the cool air washing over him. Thankfully, it was quiet enough that the young human female would not hear him.

"Your mom called when I was downstairs. She shouldn't be long. There was an accident just as she came on the route one-ninety by Death Valley Junction. That's less than half an hour away."

"Great." He needed to have a few words with his mother.

"When was the last time you saw her?" Selene took a seat at the table with him, with a small salad she'd brought for herself. No wonder she was tiny if that was all she was eating. The ice cream was good, but he couldn't wait for his mother to cook him a steak, or three or, hell, he was on holiday, make that four. Who was he kidding? He wanted the whole cow laid out on his plate. His inner leopard approved of that idea with a smacking of its lips.

"It must have been a year now. I don't get here as often as I would like."

"She said your job keeps you busy; park ranger, isn't it?"

"My mom seems to talk about me a lot," he chuckled.

"She's really proud of you." She shrugged. "I think I've pretty much seen all your baby, kindergarten, and graduation pictures, as well as all the school reports. I love the mullet you had going on in high school." It was her turn to laugh.

"Puberty hit me hard."

"You've still got a bit of a mane to you."

"This is nothing in comparison to my friend." He ran his fingers through his hair. He kept it long because it did its own thing most of the time. "He has the full fluffy thing happening, no sooner does he style it, then it goes poof into a mess again."

"Poor guy."

"What about you?"

"My hair? It does as it's told." She tucked a strand of chestnut hair behind her ear.

He raised an eyebrow at her.

"Oh, you meant who am I?"

"I did. I feel at a disadvantage. You seem to know a great deal about me."

He finished his cookies n' cream, placed the spoon back in the bowl, and popped an ice cube into his mouth to suck.

"There isn't much to know. My name is Selene Harper. I've been working for your mother for six months now, ever since I arrived in Death Valley. She's given me a room in the apartment with her. It means I can look after the place when she needs to go out."

"How old are you?"

"Twenty-one."

Throughout their entire conversation she'd been keeping eye contact with him, but now she looked down at the salad. Was that a lie? He took a deep inhalation and felt a shift in her scent. She was nervous again. There was something this human was not telling him. He would play along, for now, but when his mother returned he would be demanding answers. Who was this woman living with his mother? Was she safe with her?

"Where did you live before?" Brayden asked.

Selene put her fork down on her plate.

"Look at me stuffing my face and all I've given you is ice cream. I'll tell you what, I'll go and get a burger for you. I'm sure the chef knows how you like it." Was she deliberately avoiding his question?

"There's no need."

"No, no I insist. My lunch break is over anyway. I'll send someone up with it when it's done." She hurried out, leaving him alone with his thoughts.

His mother had emailed him a few months back asking if he would visit her, when he could get away. Brayden was the pack's lead enforcer, basically the assassin for the Glacial Blood pack. A pack, well a family really, brought together by choice, not blood. He was damned good at his job. Recently, he'd been kept busy enough that, this was the first chance he'd had to get away.

He'd bet money that whatever his mother wanted to speak to him about, it was related to the waitress. Brayden wasn't going to sit around in his mother's apartment, he was going to go down to the café and observe. His instincts were telling him something was not right here, and he'd learned at a very young age to trust them.

Brayden had just sat in the café, with his burger, when his mother arrived. He gave her a great big hug, and a contented thrum left his throat. He heard her own hum of pleasure at having her son close.

"I'm sure you've gotten even taller," his mother exclaimed and took a seat opposite him.

"Compared to Kas, I'm like an ant."

"He always was freakishly big. Your father always said it was the seal blubber. I remember the day I roasted some for him with my grandma's secret spice mix. I don't think I've ever seen a grown man drool so much with anticipation."

"Which reminds me... he wants me to bring another packet of the mix back with me. He's got a hunting trip planned."

"Please tell me he is not going to eat it raw again?" Jane raised a questioning eyebrow.

"He likes it that way," Brayden huffed.

"Philistine." His mother rolled her eyes in disgust.

Their conversation quieted when Selene brought his mother a coffee. "Thanks, Sel. How have things been?"

"No problems at all," Selene said. Brayden sat back and started on his burger while the ladies spoke. A perfect medium rare, just as he liked it.

"I see Stuart is in." His mom nodded her head towards a table full of jocks. Their team jackets were thick, despite the high temperature.

"Yes, he wants me to go out with him tonight." Selene stood with her shaking hands clasped in front of her.

"Hi, Mrs. Dillon," one of the men called out. His hair was slicked with gel into a fashionable style and he had a smug smile on his face.

"Hi, Stuart," his mom shouted back, before reverting her attention again to Selene. "I thought we might have a nice meal with Brayden?"

"I turned him down last week. I can't really say no again."

"You don't have to go out with him."

"He is good to me," Selene stated quietly.

Brayden could tell by the sudden look of disgust on his mother's face that she didn't believe that.

"And besides, you and your son probably have a lot to catch up on."

"We will do dinner tomorrow. Don't make any plans, please." There was a hint of desperation in his mother's plea.

"You have my word." Selene turned her attention to

another patron who had arrived.

"What is going on, Mom?" Brayden asked.

"We'll talk tomorrow, please. Here isn't the place."

"You are worried. We'll talk now."

Someone from the table, at which Stuart sat, loudly called over to Selene. She timidly went over to them.

"Can we get another round of sodas, please? We better get them to go. Don't want to be late for practice. Why don't you see if you can get off and come and join us?" The loud-mouthed idiot, Stuart, grabbed Selene's hand and ran his other hand up her naked leg. Instead of looking like she enjoyed it, the panic-stricken girl looked like she would be sick. A growl formed in Brayden's throat and his fingernails started to shift to claws.

"Brayden, no. She knows what she is doing." His mother placed her hand over his, hiding the sharpened talons. All he could do was watch and keep the reverberations in his throat as quiet as possible. It was his natural state; he couldn't help it. Selene nodded toward where he and his mother sat.

"I wish I could, but Miss Jane needs me." Selene removed Stuart's hand from her leg and kissed it. "But I'll be there when you finish practice, and you can show me that lookout point you wanted to. How about that?"

All Brayden could think about was, how could she be all sweetness and light when it was evident, to anyone with half a brain, that this man made her skin crawl?

"I suppose that'll do. Make sure you wear a short skirt and show me some skin. That gothic stuff you wear is awful. I never get to see anything with those long skirts."

"I think after a day here it will be a little dirty, but I will see what I can find." With that, Selene disappeared into the back and Brayden could relax. He sheathed his claws again.

"Talk, Mom." After the display he'd just witnessed he

wasn't in the mood for arguments.

"I can't here." His mother was panicked.

"Well then let's go upstairs."

"I need to check on Selene."

"Mom. What is going on?" He reached out to grab her hand, but she was too quick and got to her feet. He could see tears forming in her eyes.

"Later Brayden. Please, I need you to trust me."

"You know I do, but I can't help if I don't know what is going on." He was on his feet and round to her side of the table pulling her into his arms.

"I will tell you later, but for now, I need you to do one thing for me." She looked up at him. His mother was upset. It ruffled his leopard's fur that she was not telling him how to help.

"What?"

"Tonight, when Selene goes on her date. I need you to follow her," she asked.

"Follow her? If she wants to date that dickhead, why do I need to follow her?"

"You just do. Damn, why are you Dillon males so stubborn and need to know everything? Please, can you do what I ask for once?" This final plea was frantic.

"Ok. I'll follow her," he replied.

"Thank you. Let whatever happens, happen, but he mustn't touch her."

"Touch her? They are going to a lookout point. I'm pretty confident he plans on doing a lot more than just giving her a kiss."

"He mustn't touch her Brayden, please." His mother was serious; she was worried for this girl.

He held his hands up in surrender. "Alright. He won't."

ABOUT ANNA EDWARDS

I am a British author, from the depths of the rural countryside near London. In a previous life, I was an accountant from the age of twenty-one. I still do that on occasions, but most of my life is now spent intermingling writing while looking after my husband, two children and two cats (probably in the inverse order to the one listed!). When I have some spare time, I can also be found writing poetry, baking cakes (and eating them), or behind a camera snapping like a mad paparazzi.

I'm an avid reader who turned to writing to combat my depression and anxiety. I have a love of travelling and like to bring this to my stories to give them the air of reality.

I like my heroes hot and hunky with a dirty mouth, my heroines demure but with spunk, and my books full of dramatic suspense.

CONNECT WITH ANNA EDWARDS

www.AuthorAnnaEdwards.com

Newsletter: http://eepurl.com/cwxJ6v

Facebook, Author Page: AnnaEdwardsWriter

Facebook, Friend: TheAuthorAnnaEdwards

Twitter: @Anna__Edwards

Instagram: authorannaedwards

Pinterest: anna1000edwards

Goodreads: anna__edwards

Bookbub: @AnnaEdwards

Email: anna1000edwards@gmail.com

MEET ANNA EDWARDS

I'll be at the following signings:

2018

23rd June - When in Wales, Cardiff , UK

19-21 October – Shameless Book Convention, Showcase Author, Orlando, Florida, USA.

27th October - FanSSastic, Birmingham Airport, UK

10th November - Brighton Book Bash, Brighton, UK

2019

21-24 February - Wild Wicked Weekend, San Antonio, Texas, USA

2nd March – Leeds Author Event, Leeds, UK

1st June – Heart of Steel, Sheffield, UK.

27th July – Books on the Beach, Blackpool, UK

18-19 October – For the Love of Books & Dublin, Dublin, Ireland.

26357291R00153

Printed in Poland
by Amazon Fulfillment
Poland Sp. z o.o., Wrocław